THE BROKEN TURTLE BLUES

RUTH JOHNSON MAXWELL

© 2022 by Ruth Johnson Maxwell

All rights reserved. This book or any portion thereof may not be reproduced or used in any manner whatsoever without the express written permission of the publisher except for the use of brief quotations in a book review.

ISBN: 9798432026507 (paperback)

This is a work of fiction. Names, characters, places, and incidents are either the product of the author's imagination or are used fictitiously. Any resemblance to actual persons—living or dead—events, or locales is entirely coincidental.

Dedication

For my husband, Terry Maxwell—
my ever-patient sounding board and
never-ending source of support.

Acknowledgments

Thank you, Jennifer Lewis, for giving me an entire year of invaluable guidance and feedback as I worked to bring order to my story idea.

Deborah McComb (DM Proofreading Services) and Kate Seger (Kate Seger Proofreading Services), thanks to you both for improving my novel in a myriad of ways.

Thanks also to the following readers who provided me with much-appreciated critiques, suggestions, and encouragement throughout the writing process: Judy Schoedel, Hazel Johnson, Laurie Hancock, Brianna Johnson, Ally Johnson, Joe Johnson, Linda de Berge, Bernadine McCollum, Sandy Derau, Cathy Langley, Barbara Berg, Barbara Groy, Pepper Gearhart, Julie Wood, and Marylynne Sirutis.

And my heartfelt gratitude goes to my late sister, Cindy Smalley, and her husband, Russ, for their love and acceptance.

Chapter One

January 1995

By the time the sun appeared, January's raw northern wind gusts had all but dissipated. The small single-pane windows no longer rattled inside their flimsy aluminum frames, unraveling Ann's nerves. She allowed her head a sluggish shake, weary eyes rolling half-pikes in their sockets. With a hard yank and a "holy moly," she pulled the down comforter up to her chin, burying her hands underneath it.

Staring wide-eyed at a discolored, flower-shaped patch in the popcorn ceiling overhead, she resolved to stay awake. Soon, though, her eyes crossed, the whole bedroom becoming a fuzzy white blur. *All right, Ann Palmer, snap to it!*

Below the covers by Ann's left hip, a pillow-sized mound suddenly metamorphosed into a moving blob inching its way to freedom. She lifted the covers a sliver, chuckling as Bernie's licorice-gumdrop nose appeared and grazed her chin.

"Come here, Bernie, you lummox. The wretched wind didn't keep you up, too, did it, huh?" He crept toward her face, short floppy ears folded inside out, and planted his tongue on her nose. "Hey there, thanks for the kiss. How about we go check on Gus?"

Before summoning the courage to vacate her toasty cocoon, Ann plucked her red plastic-framed eyeglasses off the bedside table.

She peered out the frozen windowpane, running her skinny

fingers through her new pixie cut, its natural salt-and-pepper hair color a recent trial.

If only I could swap this cold Colorado weather for a few warm months in the Arizona desert. Or why not a whole mountain range flocked in this frosty 'white stuff' for one bluff and a giant saguaro? And then there's Mother! I'd gladly trade her for a dozen rattlesnakes! That's not asking for much, right?

Bernie, at best guess a cross between a basset hound and a corgi, leaped off the bed and darted out the narrow opening through the bedroom doorway.

Ann tensed, realizing that Bernie and Gus, his old littermate, would soon start roughhousing with one another. *Oh, shoot, they're gonna wake Sarah!*

She flew out from under the covers and slid across the hardwood floor in a pair of woolen ankle socks she'd put on in the middle of the night.

The guest bedroom door stood ajar.

As Ann edged closer, she spied Sarah, her younger sister, in a long turquoise T-shirt and leggings, sprawled across the bedside rug with the two troublemakers. She noted with amusement that Sarah had tucked her copper curls inside her shirt for protection from slobbery drool.

Sarah looked toward the doorway. "Well, hello, Annie, come in and join us!"

"Hey, there's the little traitor!" Ann rushed into the room, grabbing Gus around his stocky middle and hoisting him up. "My bedroom's not good enough anymore, huh?"

Wiggling around like a trout on a hook, he licked her lips, his mouth emitting a similar fish scent. "Pee-yeeeuw, your mouth smells nasty, Gus."

She allowed him a playful squeeze before placing him on the floor.

"Here, Bernie, you can have him back."

Sarah sat up. "Good heavens, the dreadful wind never let up once last night!"

"Have you forgotten how windy it gets here in the valley?" Ann asked, crossing her arms. "Of course, you haven't visited in a while. I'm glad you're here now, though." Walking over to her sister, she grabbed her hand, helping her to her feet.

"Sorry for grumbling, Sarah, but I can't help it! Even though Tim pitches in with Mother's care, I wish you'd come back more often to help me deal with her craziness. You've *always* handled her better than I have."

A deep breath did nothing to squelch the resentment settling inside Ann's chest. "I'm repeating myself, but she sucks the ever-living energy out of me. She's like an ... ogre!" She tightened her fists. "How often did we say Dad would die first and leave us to tend to Mother all alone?"

Sarah moved closer and brushed her hand over Ann's shoulder. "Yeah, good old Daddy ... we said it many times, Annie."

"The idea of wrapping oxygen tubing around her neck and giving a hard yank doesn't seem so all-fired immoral anymore! Especially when I'm lying awake in the middle of the night too tired and frustrated to sleep!" Ann flinched, half expecting to see flames shoot out her nostrils.

"Oh, Sarah," she continued, "I feel so conflicted. On the one hand, I get the guilts and feel like the horrid daughter with the giant chip on her shoulder, and other times, I think ... geez ... what can she expect, stabbing me in the gut with her diatribes my entire life?"

You've been a disappointment to me your whole life, Ann Marie! For Pete's sake, Ann Marie, straighten your hunched back, you turtle! Damn it, Ann Marie, what's wrong with you? Turtle, Turtle, Turtle!

Ann sucked in another deep breath, shaking out her hands while exhaling.

"Okay, enough whining. I'm going downstairs to check the fire and let these two yahoos out. How about we start this day with an old-fashioned, greasy breakfast?"

"Sounds like a plan," Sarah said, smiling softly as Ann backed out the doorway. "By the way, I'm glad I'm here, too ... *podunk* town and all. I promise it won't be so long between visits next time."

"Thank you."

Ann blew Sarah a kiss and turned to hide her tears.

But please don't make me beg you not to play your 'out-of-sight, out-of-mind trick' on me again. You're mighty good at it, little sis.

And I see your curvaceous bikini body's back. I forgot you vacationed in Hawaii while I shoveled snow out of Mother's driveway.

By the time Sarah had showered and come downstairs, the wood in the wood-burning stove burned so hot that the stove vibrated.

The pleasing warmth coupled with the pungent smells of fresh coffee and smoked bacon sizzling in the iron skillet worked their blessed magic. Ann's shoulders relaxed, a smile grabbing at her lips.

"Hey, Sarah, before we sit down, would you please get the newspaper? It should be somewhere out front on the porch."

"Sure. The dogs want out for another romp in the snow, okay?"

"Yep, and if we're lucky, they'll stay outside while we eat."

Sarah removed the newspaper from the plastic bag, setting it on the island.

"Thank you. Now, choose your place and pull up a stool. And would you rather have cherry jam or honey on your toast?"

"If that's the sour-cherry jam the old church lady makes for the bazaar, I'll take the jam. Yum!"

Sarah devoured her breakfast in minutes. Wiping her fingers on a leftover holiday napkin, she caught Ann's stare and grinned.

"What're you looking at? And where are you packing all that jam and toast in your teeny body, big sis?"

She laughed. "What was it that mean girl used to call you in fifth grade? Wasn't it Skinny Mini Annie Fanny?"

Ann stuck out her tongue. "And wasn't that my usual rebuttal?"

Smirking as she stacked the dirty dishes, Sarah answered, "By George, Annie, I believe so! But never to her face, as I recall!"

"True! She'd have squished me into the sidewalk like a cigarette butt. Well, not that she smoked. Although she acted tough enough."

Ann glanced at the stove clock, its grease-spattered surface in need of a Windex wipe-down. "Okay, enough clowning around. I'm going to let the dogs back in and take a look at the paper before I jump in the shower."

She hopped down from her stool, tapping Sarah's elbow with the front section of the newspaper before handing it to her. "Here! See how many names you recognize."

With an impish grin, Sarah replied, "Mm-hmm, sounds like *fun!*"

"Yep!" Ann giggled. "Anyway, as you know, things around here haven't changed much since you graduated from high school." Using the edge of her nightshirt, she wiped her eyeglasses clean. "I'm going to scan the classifieds. Tim's looking for a used band saw, and I'm dying to beat him to it. It'd make a great birthday present." Placing her hands on her hips, she resumed, "But if he knows what's good for him, he better get our outdated bedroom windows replaced first!"

And the darn popcorn ceiling needs to go, too!

Bernie and Gus made a beeline for the kitchen, scavenging the floor for crumbs while Ann scanned the For Sale ads, tracing each line with her index finger. "Whoa, Sarah, no electric saws, but look at this under Services Offered, would you?"

Ann slid the classified section across the counter to her little sis.

Sarah read out loud as Ann mouthed along. "Experienced live-in caregiver looking to relocate to the Clifton Valley/Silvermile area of South-Central Colorado to provide end-of-life care. Salary negotiable and dependent upon duties required."

Sarah raised her hand to her mouth.

"Oh, this could be your salvation, Annie!"

Ann fumbled to get the phone out of its cradle. "I know!"

Hands shaking, she dialed the numbers as Sarah called them out.

"It's ringing! Oh, darn, it's going to voicemail. Come on, beep. Hurry up! Okay, there it goes ... Hello, my name's Ann Palmer, and I'm calling in regard to your caregiver ad in this week's *Clifton Valley News*. My 89-year-old mother, Mabel Castle, is in the final stage of emphysema and refuses to go into a nursing home. Um ... she's presently in the hospital but should be released soon. Anyway, my sister and I would be interested in talking with you. Thank you." Ann hung up the phone.

"Great, Annie. You forgot to leave your phone number."

"Oh, no! She should have Caller ID, shouldn't she?"

"I suppose. Go take your shower, and I'll clean up the kitchen." Sarah rolled up the sleeves of her corduroy shirt—the same emerald color as her stirring green eyes. "We can try again after you get dressed."

"Okay, I won't be long."

Sarah scraped her bread crusts into the garbage and rinsed off the dinnerware before loading the dishwasher. Suddenly, the phone rang, causing her to jump. "Come on; pick up the phone, Annie."

After hearing her sister answer upstairs, Sarah turned her attention to the messy countertops.

As she rummaged through the drawer of kitchen linens for a dishrag, Ann came barreling down the stairs, damp hair plastered to her scalp like an old-time swim cap.

"The caregiver called us back already, Sarah! She wants to meet us today at two o'clock for a late lunch, and I suggested the new café by the barbershop."

"Yeah, I heard the phone ring. She didn't waste any time."

"Nope, she didn't." Ann wiped her wet hands across her robe and raced over to the stove clock. "Okay, we have a few hours, but there's so much to do. Um ... I'll wear my long denim skirt and—"

"Slow down, Annie. You're dripping all over the place. Go dry your hair while I finish up in the kitchen. Did you at least get her name?"

"Yes, of course, I did. Even though I'm losing my mind by taking care of Mother, I'm not a moron. Her name's Larita Moretti, and she lives in West Denver. She's been an in-home caregiver for ten years and promised to bring a list of references."

"All right, fair enough."

Ann did a victory dance at the base of the stairs, knees high and fists in the air, before leaping up the steps two at a time.

Shaking her head, Sarah shouted up the stairs. "You're like an overexcited child, Annie! You better realize we can't make a snap decision this afternoon! We need to think this through and check out her references!"

"Yep, I know!" *But don't you dare poop on my parade, sister dear!*

■ ■ ■

The sisters climbed into Ann's Jeep Cherokee and drove the short distance to their mother's two-story log home. After checking on Rufus and Sassy—Mabel's overweight, aged tabby cats—and doing a routine cleanup, the duo again slid into the Cherokee and backed out of the snow-packed driveway.

The snowplow had cleared Center Street, allowing Ann to zip through Clifton Valley's single stoplight, a usual source of amusement for Sarah. The two arrived minutes later at a front-row parking spot near the entrance to the Boss Cat Café.

"You're lucky to still live here in Clifton, Annie. Traffic and noise in Ranston keep getting worse as Salt Lake City continues to expand. If Mom weren't an issue and I could find work, I'd consider moving back."

"There's an immediate opening for an *ambivalent* caregiver! And a certain pediatric nurse would get first dibs! Interested?"

"You're a laugh a minute, Annie. I hope you choke on your burger!"

"And leave you all alone to deal with Mother?" The two exchanged a high five.

The loud idling of a motorcycle pulling into the adjacent parking space muffled their merriment. The two watched as a slight figure dressed in black leather dismounted and engaged the kickstand.

"Could that be the caregiver?" Sarah asked.

"I doubt it ... probably a small guy."

Sarah cocked her head to the side. "That's true. Either way, the main roads must be cleared off, or our mystery rider's suicidal." She unsnapped her seatbelt and straightened her wool poncho. "You want to wait inside the café where it's warm?"

"Sure." Ann grabbed her purse from behind the driver's seat. "No need to lock up. But hey, before we go in, please remember how much Tim and I need this reprieve. I'd rather have all my teeth extracted without anesthesia than continue providing Mother's care. And that's barely an exaggeration."

"Sarah leaned over the console and gave Ann a much-appreciated squeeze.

"Constantly dealing with Mom's got to be a nightmare, Annie. And I'd like to help." She sat back in her seat. "So may I suggest we pour on the *Fred Castle* charm over lunch? Daddy could charm anyone; sometimes even Mom. Remember?"

"Yep, I ... oh, no, look at my watch, it's after two. We'd better get inside."

The lunch crowd had long gone; at most, a few stragglers remained.

As Ann and Sarah stepped through the doorway, a small table of Ann's church friends waved. The owner, new to town, picked up two menus from behind the counter and introduced himself, offering a brawny hand to both women.

Sarah took hold of the menus. "Thank you. And we're waiting for another party to join us, so we'll need an extra one."

"Excuse me," said a voice from behind, "I'm Larita Moretti. I couldn't help but overhear—"

Sarah and Ann spun around and stared, mouths agape, as they learned that the leather-clad motorcycle rider was, indeed, Mabel's potential caregiver.

Underneath the heavy jacket, now unzipped, she wore a red-and-gray flannel shirt, unbuttoned and tied in a knot at her waist. The opening framed a tattoo of muted butterflies and script accentuated by the scoop neck of a bright-white T-shirt.

A long turquoise earring dangled from her left ear, her waist-length, glossy black hair covering the other.

"Gosh, please excuse my poor manners." Ann willed the exclamation mark off her face while shaking Larita's hand. "My name's

Ann Palmer. I'm the one you spoke with this morning, and this is my sister, Sarah Castle."

"Nice to meet you both," Larita said, offering Sarah a firm handshake. "I'm sitting in the booth by the big window. Okay?"

"Sure, looks great," replied Sarah.

The two sisters sat side by side on the tufted vinyl booth across from the caregiver. A fanciful collection of 1960s memorabilia—from record album covers to metal lunchboxes and board games—spanned the shelves and walls, providing fodder for small talk. With orders taken, Ann caught Larita's attention.

"Well, Mother's ... um ... colorful, to say the least. Sarah will agree that life with Mabel Castle's never dull. She's like a ... banty rooster," Ann said, squirming around like a timid teenager, "small but feisty. And believe me, growing up on a farm—"

Sarah cast a side-glance at her sister. "Good heavens, Annie, quit beating around the bush!" She turned her attention to Larita. "Truth be told, Mom's downright nasty sometimes. And other times, she's tolerable ... even lets her sense of humor rip loose." She glanced at Ann once again. "We both need to be straightforward with you."

Ann's face grew as red as the cherry-colored seat. "Yes, you're right, Sarah."

Thanks a bunch. I'm doing a terrific job of appearing like an idiot without your help.

"Ladies, you've piqued my interest. But first, I have to admit I'm a glutton for the meanings of given names. Do you have any idea what the name Mabel means?"

Without hesitating, Sarah answered, "Having narcissistic tendencies and a Jekyll-and-Hyde personality! What do you think, Annie?"

"Add overbearing, and you've nailed it, Sarah!"

Larita laughed, a warm smile planted on her lips. "Nope, I'm afraid not. I have a dear friend named Mabel and happen to know the name Mabel is of English origin and means *lovable*."

Spitting water into the air like Old Faithful, Sarah swallowed hard and set her glass on the table with a loud *thud*. "Obviously, our grandparents didn't bother to check her name's origin. I mean, she must have possessed her fiery temper at birth! I'd bet everything I own on it."

"Okay, ladies, I hate to be a party pooper, but what's your mother's prognosis? Ann, you mentioned emphysema on the phone."

"Yes. The doctors indicate that she's in the 'severe stage.' As soon as she knocks one lung infection, another follows. Even with oxygen, her breathing's labored. And she's been on oxygen for five years. Right, Sarah?"

"Something like that. Anyway, the doctor says she'll be well enough to leave the hospital by the weekend. And she also has type-2 diabetes, which will require daily testing and insulin."

"Bah! Her diabetes diagnosis was quite a surprise!" Ann said. "I took her to a doctor's appointment one morning when Dad wasn't feeling well, and the doctor asked me how she'd adapted to her diabetic diet. Dumfounded, I said, 'Her *what*?'"

She shrugged. "Of course, he looked at me like I was an idiot."

Sarah and Larita laughed.

Ann wasn't done yet, though.

"Neither Mother nor Dad had mentioned a special diet. Let alone diabetes. Until then, most of the meals my husband Tim and I had taken over to Mother weren't fit for a diabetic ... a queen, maybe—"

"And a queen she isn't," Sarah added, "though she thinks she is."

Ann chuckled. "Yes, she certainly does. And when Tim had

done the cooking up until that point, you'd have thought she was a queen! Geez, he can cook, even looks like those cute, tubby, bald Italian chef figurines for sale in the cooking stores all over Denver. Although not as tubby or bald."

Catching Sarah's impatient grimace, Ann cringed.

A deflated "blah, blah, blah," passed through her lips and hovered over the table. "And there's little dementia at this point, for Mabel, I mean."

Ann waited for their courtesy laugh and eyed Sarah. "I'm digressing here, aren't I? What's wrong with me today?"

Sarah patted her sister's leg. "You're exhausted, Annie." Breathing deeply, she turned toward Larita. "Anyway, if you decide to give the job a try, you'd have the whole upstairs of Mom's house to yourself, along with free room and board, plus your salary, of course."

Sarah, kudos on your pitch! I underestimated you.

Ann sat upright in the booth, as straight as her bent spine allowed.

"Tim and I live down the road less than a mile," she said, "and we'll continue lending a hand."

Larita tilted her head, brows drawn.

"Well, the job sounds appealing, a good challenge. But how about we find out what your mom wants?"

Ann and Sarah stared at each other, open-mouthed.

The trio burst into laughter, all tension dissolved.

Afterward, discussions ranged from the local real estate market and tourist attractions to Larita's recent Alaskan trip with long-time friends.

Later, the three women headed toward the community hospital in the neighboring town of Silvermile—eighteen miles southwest of Clifton Valley—following a quick stop at Mabel's to park Larita's motorcycle and show her the layout.

By now, the state's snowplow crews had worked the narrow two-lane roadway a second time, leaving it clear and dry in spots.

■ ■ ■

Mabel appeared lost among the drab hospital linens lying in uneven waves up to her chin. Even from the doorway, Ann could see that her wispy, white hair needed a trim. Like a great white shark, Mabel's piercing, dark eyes spotted her visitors at once.

"It looks like your roommate left," Sarah said, approaching the bed. "Annie told me her name was Alice." She lowered the side rail. "I haven't seen you in a while. How are you doing today?"

A deep scowl erupted across Mabel's forehead.

With an impatient *humph,* she removed her arms from underneath the top sheet, her thin, taut skin a shiny black and blue. Hand trembling, she pointed to her right ear, indicating the need for her hearing aids.

Sarah picked up the waxy plastic knobs and checked the batteries. She placed herself in Mabel's line of vision.

"Do you want to put them in, or do you want me to do it?"

With a slack look of indifference, Mabel gazed at her lap, refusing to look at Sarah. "I want the girl you brought with you to do it."

Sarah grinned at her sister. Silently mouthing the words, she said, "Someone new to torture."

Without hesitation, Larita walked up to the bedside and picked up Mabel's frail hands, cradling them. "Hi, Mabel, my name's Larita. I'd be happy to put in your hearing aids."

Mabel's dour face brightened with the attention.

Eating it up, huh, Mother? Well, keep 'eating'! It's time somebody else 'fed' you!

As Larita finished adjusting the hearing aids, Sarah walked around to the other side of the bed.

"One, two…three," she said as she and Larita lifted Mabel up toward the headboard, straightening her pillows and linens.

The movement brought on a series of deep coughs and a mouthful of phlegm.

Larita helped Mabel spit into a tissue.

"Guess who I had lunch with today, Mabel?"

Mabel's face pinched into a scowl.

"Lunch? Well, how should I know?"

Larita ignored the bitter retort and smiled, throwing the used tissue into the trashcan.

"Then I'll tell you. I had lunch today with *your girls* before they brought me here to meet you."

Mabel leaned forward, eyes glued to Larita's face.

For a change, she seemed eager to discover something.

Eager and interested.

"They'd like for me to move into your house and help take care of you and your sweet cats, Sassy and Rufus. Would that be all right? If I helped your daughters, you'd be able to go home soon, back to where you want to be. What do you think?"

"Fine." Mabel's scowl reappeared. "I don't get a say in anything anyway."

Ann's eyebrows rose. *For goodness' sake, Mother, we just gave you 'a say.'* A side-glance from Larita stopped her from replying to Mabel's comment. Larita's expression seemed to convey that she'd be taking over Mabel's care.

"Now, fetch my clothes and get me out of here!" Mabel said to Larita in her usual demanding tone. Her eyes narrowed, and her attention shifted to Ann. Barking out the order as if she believed the nurse had deliberately hidden her clothes, she said, "Ann Marie, show her where the darn nurse stashed 'em!"

Ann's heart did a summersault in appreciation for a just reward. Bouncing on her toes, she reached forward and touched Sarah's elbow. In a hushed voice, she asked, "Does this mean what I hope it means?"

Sarah nodded in double time, and Ann sensed by Larita's attentiveness to Mother that she'd made the same realization.

"Wait a minute, Mabel," Larita said. She held her new client's hands, catching her gaze. "We need to slow down a bit. I have to go home to Denver and pack my bags. And you need to get stronger so the doctor can discharge you. Okay?"

Continuing in her indignant vein, head wagging, Mabel asked, "Is that so?"

Larita remained calm. "Yes, Miss Mabel."

All three visitors struggled to stifle their laughs as Mabel's shrill voice bit into her new caregiver's words. "Yes, Miss Mabel!"

I hope Larita understands what she'll be dealing with. Heaven help her!

Larita's smile broadened. She seemed to enjoy every minute spent with the cantankerous old fussbudget.

Chapter Two

May 1996

The afternoon had wound down. Ann returned to her mother's estate for the day's final round of sorting, following a quick dash home to let Bernie and Gus outside one last time. After tossing her jean jacket across the arm of the couch, she pushed up the sleeves of her top and surveyed the scattered piles of photographs.

Disappointed by how little headway she'd made today, she closed her eyes tight, balled up her fists, and let out a low-pitched yowl.

"Why on earth, Mother, did you die and leave me alone to deal with this mess?" She cradled her head and sucked in the room's stale air. *Okay, drama queen, get a hold of yourself and grab a pile of these photos.*

Partway through the stack, Ann's scowl melted like the heavy snowpack receding up Mt. Polk's jagged west face, visible outside the picture window above the couch. *All right, there's Dad and me with Mother's cocky old rooster. What was his name?*

She brought the photo closer and hollered. "Hey, Tim, can you break away for a minute? I have a few photos to show you."

He answered in a loud voice, "Sure, give me a second. I could use a break. Didn't even hear you return."

Ann cupped her hands around her mouth. "Sorry, I should've told you I'm back! I'm on the floor in front of the couch!"

Tim tossed the travel magazines he'd already sorted through

into the makeshift recycle bin in Mabel's former bedroom. Stepping sideways, he squeezed past the dozens of boxes not yet organized, all lining the narrow hallway.

Rounding the corner into the family room, he chuckled. "Where are you? I can't see you for all this stuff!"

Ann replied with an all-too-common groan, "I know. Even I can't tell if I'm making headway. Here, I'll move the remaining photos so you can sit by me."

He lowered himself onto the tatty Berber carpet, grumbling like a cold engine refusing to start. "Ugh! My cup-half-full attitude's gone."

"Well, we need to vow to one another that we're never going to do this to Katie. Never leave her with enough crap to furnish a dozen households."

"And a thrift store, to boot. Yes, I promise," Tim said with a facetious smile, flashing the Boy Scouts' three-finger salute.

"Good, good, good!" *'Good' heavens, that is! And it's a 'good' thing Katie's at college and doesn't have to witness this mess!*

"So, what's up?"

Amusement flickered in Ann's eyes. "I'd like to show you a few pictures taken when I was a kid. Since you're such a good sport!"

"Uh-huh ... okay, bring 'em on."

Tim scooted nearer, adjusting his reading glasses.

"Here's Dad with me on top of his shoulders." Ann fingered his image. "He was a good-looking man, wasn't he? As tall and strapping as ... the folk story guy with the blue ox ... oh ... Paul Bunyan. Yeah."

She scanned the photo.

"Hmm, the trees are bare. It must've been taken in early spring or late fall. I was, what, three or four here?" She pointed to her image. "Ha! I'm wearing the itchy wool headscarf Mother always made me wear so I wouldn't 'catch cold.' Sarah had one, too."

Ann lowered the snapshot.

"It wasn't until first or second grade that I understood I could stash the horrid *thing* in my coat pocket when Mother wasn't around."

She clapped her hands in delight. "Ha! I remember how she used to make us wear long pants under our dresses during the winter! Gawd, we must've looked like ragamuffins."

"No doubt," Tim replied with a chuckle.

"So, Mr. Palmer, you bored yet?"

"Nah, Mrs. Palmer. Your *ramblings* beat the heck out of sorting through this junk."

Ann nudged him with her elbow. "Good to hear! Now, getting back to Dad."

She raised the photograph for one last glance.

"The world must've looked pretty impressive sitting on his shoulders." *Too bad we didn't spend more time together, though; he certainly had the market cornered on business trips!* "And here's old ... Attaboy ... yeah, that was his name." Pointing to the rooster's clear, black-and-white likeness, she said, "Sounds more like an affectionate dog's name, but he truly was one mean chicken. He scared the *bejeebers* out of me."

Her body shuddered. "Anyway, before we'd go into Attaboy's pen, Dad would have me wrap my arms around his neck while he shielded himself from attack with the lid to the barrel of chicken feed. In one fluid motion, he'd have the water changed, the feeder filled, and we'd be backing out the gate."

"Sarah was a baby then, right?"

"Yeah." Ann turned the snapshot over. "Good, it's dated. Let me see ... sometimes it's hard to read Mother's writing with all its loop-the-loops." She squinted. "It says it was taken by Grandma Castle on Sarah's first birthday, March 15, 1960. I would've been three-and-a-half years old."

"That's right," Tim said, slowly nodding. "You're two-and-a-half years older." He handed over several random photos from the pile in front of Ann. "And these?"

"Oh, how funny! That's me—Miss Hooligan," she said, pointing at the taller figure. "Sarah was named ... uh ... Miss Calhoun. Look at those oh-so-stylish hats and gaudy pocketbooks, as Mother called them. Didn't we make cute little old ladies?"

"Our favorite part of playing dress-up was 'smoking' those candy cigarettes we're holding. We thought we were so cool." She held up her 'smoking' hand to demonstrate. "We'd hold the nasty sugar sticks between our index and middle fingers—like this—and deeply inhale before blowing out a pretend puff of smoke. It's hard to believe neither one of us took up smoking as teens."

Tim squinted at the picture, trying to get a better look at his Miss Hooligan.

"And this one," she said, placing this third picture on top of the other two. "I still regret what happened to Batman. Remember that story?"

"Nope, can't say as I do."

"Well, after bugging Mother for days, she caved in and let me keep this tiny, abandoned chick Sarah and I had named after our favorite *caped crusader* next to my bed. But only if I promised not to remove it from its special box that Mother had fixed with a heating pad on the bottom to keep the chick warm." Ann tapped the photo. "But did I listen?"

"My guess would be no."

"Yep ... you're right; I didn't. I put the baby chicken in bed with me and fell asleep on it. It was as lifeless and flat as a hockey puck the next morning. I'd killed the poor thing and cried for days." Tim gave her shoulder a pat, unable to stifle a loud snort.

"Sure, go ahead and laugh," she said with a half-smile. "Believe it or not, Mother never yelled at me much or said 'I told you so.' At least not that I remember. Instead, she removed the carcass and ignored me for eons. But that was the norm. The ignoring part, I mean. Of course, she also did her fair share of yelling."

"You know that, though." Ann cocked her head, painful memories distorting her face.

As well as taking a switch to my bare skin more than a time or two. And I suppose I can't leave out the name-calling either.

She shook the tension from her body before standing.

"Here, let me turn on the table lamp. We should head home anyway. I'm tired. I bet you are, too."

"Yeah, I'm glad I have to return to work tomorrow."

"Party pooper!" Ann crossed her arms. "Actually, I have a few more boxes I'd like to sort through tonight. Maybe I'll take 'em home and sort 'em out there." She patted his hand. "In fact, would you please grab the biggest one by the back door? Watch the bottom, though; it doesn't look too sturdy."

"Sure, Miss Hooligan … or should I call you *Killer*?"

"All right, mister wiseass! I'm going to lock up. I'll be home in a few minutes," she said, taking off her glasses and rubbing the bridge of her nose. "Oh, and why don't we fix the pepperoni pizza that's in the freezer? There're also salad-makings left over from last night. Okay?"

"Sure, I'll toss the pizza in the oven. Maybe throw on a couple more toppings. See you in a few minutes."

Ann watched Tim through the kitchen window as he loaded the box into the back end of their dark-green Subaru—named

Slug—and backed out of Mabel's old driveway. Thankful mid-May had arrived, she gazed at the new leaves clothing the pale, naked aspen tree branches.

She'd been sorting through the estate since Mother Nature dropped thirty-two inches of snow last Halloween. Ann needed to finish organizing the household items. Her parents' old collections had all but swallowed the home's 1,800-square-foot interior and consisted of: pig figurines—143 at last count; sanding planes; paperweights, many straight from the Fenton Art Glass factory in Williamstown, West Virginia; vintage marbles; political campaign buttons dating back to 1916; fishing lures; railroad memorabilia; vintage clothing irons; antique hair curling irons; and this, that, and the other forged from wrought iron, including dozens of old branding irons.

Once she could cross the house off her to-do list, she'd tackle the two-car garage.

Inside the garage, more treasures—embedded inside countless boxes of junk that towered higher than Ann could reach—awaited discovery. At last, it would be down to sorting out the two-story barn and assorted outbuildings.

Ann's saving grace remained the fact that Sarah had arranged to take a two-week leave of absence from work to help finish the sorting before the big three-day auction planned for mid-August.

Meanwhile, she'd have to fight the urge to shut her eyes and fill the commercial dumpster parked in the driveway rather than continue working with this dogged diligence.

Returning to the task at hand, Ann knelt in front of the couch and gathered all but one mountain of pictures. These, she pushed underneath for safekeeping. Before standing, she thumbed through the remaining photographs and selected one. "Oh, there's Lucky... what a wonderful horse!"

Ann's shoulders dropped. "Great! Now I'm talking out loud to myself!"

Okay, that's it. I'm through.

■ ■ ■

As Ann bent over to set down the boxes of office supplies from her mother's estate on her front deck, she spotted Larita's Harley. Before she grabbed hold of the doorknob, Larita burst through the door and gave her a hug.

"Hello, Miss Annie! It's great to see you."

"You, too! When did you get back into town?"

"A few days ago. I even signed a lease today on a small place north of Silvermile on several wooded acres. You'll have to help me set up house."

"Of course, I'd like that."

Larita bent down. "Here, let me get the boxes. Tim's waiting for the pizza to heat up and invited me to stay for a slice."

"Yeah, well, he better have," Ann said with a giggle, stepping through the doorway. "Thanks for the help."

While Larita set the boxes down, Ann tossed the loose photos she'd stashed in her coat pocket on the top of the dining table and pulled out two chairs.

Tim grabbed a stool from the kitchen island and joined them.

"How's the little college student?" Larita asked

"Not as homesick since Sassy and Rufus, those poor tub-of-lard cats, are there to keep Katie company in her apartment," answered Tim. "She seems to be doing all right ... good grades her second semester. The last we heard, she plans to take a few summer classes while continuing to waitress. Of course, as soon as she learns you're back, she'll be racing home for a visit."

Larita chuckled. "I'm counting on it!"

Ann bent forward and placed her hands on Larita's forearms. "Not to change the subject, but you look fantastic—rested and full of energy. Where's your secret potion? Tim and I could use a swig."

"What we need to do is get our rear ends outside and go for walks again, Annie. Couldn't hurt." Tim tapped his slight, middle-aged paunch.

Ann looked at Tim with raised eyebrows. "Yeah, well, remember the big 'C'-word—commitment? No excuses!"

A smile brightened Larita's eyes. "True on both counts, guys. One of my greatest passions is walking. But look who I'm talking to ... needless to say, you two remember that."

She suddenly appeared deep in thought, twisting her bracelet around in circles.

"I was able to walk at Gilda's, too," Larita continued, "the elderly woman I took care of after Mabel. Anytime her family would drop by during the day, her dachshund and I would make the two-mile loop around the neighborhood."

She rubbed her chin and said in a low, pouty voice, "Dadgummit, I miss that little dog! I contemplated adopting him, although I wouldn't have known what to do with him when a job required me to stay in a client's home. Anyway, Gilda, the sweet soul, passed on several weeks ago."

A devious grin touched Tim's dimples. "I bet Gilda was a pleasant distraction after Mabel—the mother-in-law from ... well, you know where."

Ann snorted and tapped Larita's knee.

"That's why you look so ... hmm ... should I say *chipper?* I get it now. You switched from nasty old Mabel to sweet little Gilda in one fell swoop. No wonder!"

And as for you, Tim, you better watch what you say about Mother. She'd be the kind to haunt us. Gawd, can you imagine!

Larita scooted her seat forward. "Gosh, I can't believe I nearly forgot to tell you my Mabel-Harley story! I hope I can spit it out before the pizza's done."

She glanced at the oven timer. "Well, as you know, Mabel relished having the last word on everything, and the day of her memorial service was no exception. I was on my way to Denver, checking my watch—the two o'clock starting time on my mind—and at the exact moment the hour hand reached the two, the Harley sputtered and *stopped*. I had to push the darn thing off the road!"

"You can't be serious," Ann said with an amused smile.

"Dead serious. And no pun intended! I checked the gas gauge first, but the tank was half full. Next, I looked at the petcock to be certain it was turned to 'run,' and it was. So I sat there, thinking through a few more possibilities. Then, five minutes later, it started right up, and I was back on the road." With a head bob, Larita said, "I believe Mabel thoroughly enjoyed having this one last poke at me."

Ann burst into laughter. "And no more problems after that?"

"None."

As if on cue, the oven buzzer sounded. Larita dug into her pizza, anxious to get out back and give attention to Bernie and Gus, her old four-legged walking buddies.

"You know, Annie," she said between bites, "you ought to jot down the stories behind these photos on the table. It's amazing how bits and pieces of information are lost over the years."

Tim nodded, mouth downturned. "Yep, that's true, even entire stories. I could kick myself for not recording my dad's boyhood stories or those about his WWII experiences." He smiled, chuckling. "He'd been dubbed the barracks' prankster more than once. Anyway, he met my mom during his stint in the army."

"Oh, yeah. She was a USO singer, right?" asked Ann.

"Yes. Lots of stories there, too. If only I'd have used a tape recorder."

"Hey, we both believed there'd be a tomorrow, my dear. And I imagine most people hold that same belief."

Larita glanced at her friends with an encouraging smile. "Mmhmm, they sure do, guys."

Tim slid off the stool and set his dishware in the sink. "Take your time, ladies; I'm gonna clean up the counters."

"Thanks, Tim," said Ann, her mouth half full.

After swallowing her last sip of iced tea, Larita leaned forward.

In a whisper, she said, "You found a good one in him, Miss Annie, and vice versa." She patted Ann's hand. "At any rate, jotting down those stories might be a good way to put the past into perspective ... and give you ... let's say ... greater freedom to move forward. Think it over, will you?"

Larita placed her drinking glass and fork on her plate and walked over to the dishwasher. "Mind if I go out back and see 'the boys'?" she asked Tim. "I don't want to be a spoilsport, but I better head home before it turns pitch black."

"No, of course, please do," he replied, motioning toward the back door.

Before Ann could pry herself away from the table, Tim had the kitchen back in order. She swung her legs over the side of the chair and looked in his direction, Larita's suggestion running figure eights inside her brain.

"It seems like a feasible project, Tim. I'd have to confiscate the kitchen table for a while, though—use it as my workstation. It's no big deal eating dinners at the island, is it?"

"Huh? You've lost me. What're you talking about?"

"Larita's idea to write down the stories behind Mother's

pictures and, maybe," she said, shoulders raised, "even our photos. I could start after the auction. It'd be something to occupy my time during the winter."

"Yeah, it sounds reasonable enough."

"Good. In the meantime, I can organize Mother's pictures into albums and make a few notes."

I'll have to let the photos do the talking ... really listen to 'em. Let 'em fill in the parts I don't clearly remember.

Ann turned back around in her seat, facing the table, and plucked a half-dozen of the black-and-white snapshots from the tabletop.

"With duplicates to choose from, I can also fill albums for Sarah and Katie. Surely these old photos will bring back memories worth writing down. Certain ones ... not so pleasant, but what the heck? Larita's right; the project might even be therapeutic."

Didn't she say something about past memories making splendid teachers?

Ann peeled herself off the chair and walked over to the sink while Tim wrung out the dishrag. "Like this one when I was in first grade at Box Elder Elementary." She waited for him to dry his hands and handed him the picture. "Look at the old brick school building. I remember those huge floodlights above the doorway. They gave me the creeps, peering at me like bulging frog eyes on the lookout for a meal."

She raised her finger. "But the snake incident ranked as the top school story for us kids. Well, the *two* snake incidents, I should say. School hadn't been in session for more than a month—"

Chapter Three

September 1964 - August 1967

First-grade students at Box Elder Elementary School failed to notice the first screams as they traveled up from the basement, losing volume by the time they'd reached the second-story classroom. Instead, the children sat at their desks, absorbed in the stories printed in their newly distributed readers.

Later that afternoon, a second series of screams—this time, sharp and chilling—brought the students to their feet moments before the final bell.

Hurried footsteps and a boy's winded voice echoed down the drab upstairs hallway and through the open slats in the classroom door.

"Guess what? Betty Smithum just saw a *huge* snake and peed her pants!"

A second boy roared with laughter.

"How funny! Let's go tell everybody on the playground!"

An explosion of chatter ignited inside the first-grade classroom. Animated faces and flailing extremities whirled around Betty Smithum's red-faced kid sister while the boys in the back of the room laughed at the sniffling, crumpled-up girl in the front.

"Okay, class; let's not get too excited," Mrs. Fletcher said from her desk. "Please, get your lunchboxes off the shelf and line up single file at the door. I'm sure Principal Hodges has the situation under control."

The children struggled to contain their giddy whispers as they learned that this second bull snake had slithered in through a small window opening in the girls' basement lavatory.

Ann turned around, facing the girl behind her, and said in a hushed voice, "My dad showed me a big, ole bull snake one time. It was really neat. But I kinda wish I woulda seen this one."

The girl's face beamed. "Uh-huh, me, too! I've never seen one before."

Ann scrunched up her cheeks. "Maybe, 'cause it's hot outside, the poor, ole snake wanted to hang out somewhere cooler."

Remarkably, the following week Ann found herself in a new first-grade classroom at another elementary school situated in the opposite direction from her house.

She never did learn if her mother's decision to have her transferred transpired because of the two snake incidents. But the next two years resulted in two more grade school shuffles and two more occasions in which to make new friends.

■ ■ ■

Ann's hunched stance had worsened by the time she entered third grade, although Dr. Stiller, her pediatrician, held little concern. He'd said, "She's like a shy turtle pulling itself into its shell, but as she matures and develops more self-confidence, she'll shed her *psychological* shell, and her back will appear normal once again."

"Well, it darn well better!" had been Mabel's haughty reply. "No child of mine would dare go through life embarrassing me by looking like a confounded turtle!"

In the meantime, Mabel reminded Ann to stand up straight, often taunting "Turtle" as she ground her bony thumb back and forth between the vertebrae in her eldest daughter's hunched upper back.

Ann, the good little soldier, responded by pulling her shoulders back, obedient and eager to win her mother's meager affections. However, this stance remained only partially effective as it made her skinny frame look stiff and awkward and vanished when she no longer concentrated on her efforts.

Relaxed and preoccupied, her shoulders again became rounded, shoulder blades protruding outward like scrawny chicken wings.

Third grade also brought with it ever-protruding front teeth and blue cat-eye glasses that hid Ann's sable eyes and long lashes. A small group of older grade-school bullies often hurled names at her like four eyes and beaver teeth.

Even so, Ann found solace among a close-knit circle of other socially awkward kids at Dalhart Elementary. She even 'married' a fellow classmate, Phillip, in his family's basement during a mock ceremony when his parents were next door.

"I need flowers for my ... *bride's flower thingy*," Ann said, holding up a finger. "How about the fake tulips in the kitchen? I'll be right back." As she dashed upstairs, her sandals clattered against the wooden steps.

"And I guess we need rings, too. Hmm ... I know," Phillip said to Terry, his best friend. "Dad throws his cigar bands in his office trashcan."

Minutes later, Terry—assuming the role of the minister—stood in front of the couple.

"All right, put on the rings," he said, chuckling.

Phillip pulled two foil cigar bands from his front pants pocket and handed one to Ann. "Here, you're supposed to put this one on my finger."

Terry turned to the couple. "I now ... call you husband and wife!" He cringed and added in a whisper, "Even though it's kinda creepy!"

Phillip planted a peck on the bride's cheek, making her giggle. Their innocent infatuation lasted throughout the entire school year.

Poor Ann didn't yet know that her fourth-grade year would take place miles away in a brand new elementary school located much closer to her family's small farm.

■ ■ ■

While living on their country farm provided Ann and Sarah with captivating outbuildings to conquer and an animal army to help care for, the remote location made it difficult to play with friends. Instead, the girls filled their summers playing with each other. Mud pies, Matchbox cars, Army men, and Barbie dolls all competed for their attention. Ann, more so than her younger sister, liked to spend time outdoors, especially when tending to Shorty, her pony.

Shorty had a full-grown colt named Rollo, who'd become Sarah's pony by default. Rather than trudging through the barnyard muck, though, Sarah preferred to put on an apron and help Mabel roll out sugar cookie dough and pie crusts or cream the frosting for a German chocolate cake.

On a lazy summer afternoon in early June, between Ann's third- and fourth-grade years, she decided to give Sarah another riding lesson on Shorty. Since Rollo was green broke (incompletely trained) and had an ornery temperament, heaving Sarah up onto his back remained nonnegotiable—especially if Ann hoped to avoid her mother's wrath.

"Come on, Sarah, I'll help you up."

Ann bent over and cupped both hands to form a stirrup.

Sarah stood on tiptoes, grabbing the reins with one hand and a thick fistful of coarse mane with the other. As Ann pushed upward, Sarah's right leg swung over Shorty's bare back.

"Why can't you put the saddle on?" Sarah asked, voice pinched.

"Because it's more fun to ride bareback, that's why." Sarah kept hold of the reins as her sister let go of the bridle and stepped back.

"Now, kick with both heels and click your tongue."

Sarah did as instructed, but Shorty stood in place, long tail swishing the air.

"Kick harder!"

Still, the only movement remained the mare's tail, its swishing picking up pace.

"Here," Ann said, smacking Shorty's hindquarters with her hand, dust flying.

Shorty lurched forward in a wink before making an abrupt turn. Sarah dropped the reins and slid off. With a *thud*, she landed on her left side, winded, arm protruding at an odd angle from underneath her head.

Ann screamed Sarah's name and sailed the short distance across the barren ground. Frantic at the commotion, the mare tore back to the barn at a dead run.

Ann placed her face close to Sarah's.

Something deep inside told her not to move her little sis, whose glassy eyes brimmed with tears.

"Please don't budge! I'm going to run to the house and get Mom. I'll be right back. I promise!" Fighting back tears, she said, "I'm sorry, Sarah!"

Mabel wasted no time. She threw the frayed tea towel she'd embroidered years ago across the bowls stacked in the dish drainer and dashed to the back door, slipping into her *clodhoppers*—a beat-up pair of tennis shoes without the laces. "You can't stay away from trouble, huh, Ann Marie? What's wrong with you? Ewwww, if only your uncle—"

Ann stood back and pointed to Sarah. "She's over by the old garden! I'm sorry, Mom!"

Sarah's left arm had swelled and her face—painted with dust and tears—appeared pale and contorted by pain. She remained still as her mother made a quick assessment. The farm's remote location prohibited a speedy ambulance response.

Instead, Mabel planned to transport Sarah to the hospital in the back of their station wagon. She scoured through the downed fencing that had once framed the old garden beds for a makeshift stretcher.

The rotting cedar gate would have to do.

Ann watched in silence as their mother slid Sarah onto the gate, careful to keep her limbs immobile. Mabel ran her hand across Sarah's forehead. "Hang in there ... not much longer. You're my brave little girl."

Ann knelt by her sister's side while Mabel fetched the Rambler station wagon from the driveway. Moments later, with her tongue protruding from the side of her mouth like a winded dog's, she attempted to help guide the gate into the car's backend.

"Now, go put your blasted horse away!" Mabel raised an open palm. "And you better hop to it, missy, because I've got a good mind to slap the tar out of you! You make my skin crawl."

Shorty stood outside the corral fence, nibbling on a stray clump of crested wheat. Breathless, Ann wrapped the reins around the pony's neck and pulled up. "Geez, Shorty, you could've killed her! And now Mom's gonna kill us both!" She swung the metal gate open, removed Shorty's bridle, and shooed her inside. "Wait till we get back from the hospital!" Ann glanced sidelong at the mare before dashing across the gravel, her steps quickening as the car horn sounded.

Before long, the jiggly, pumpkin-colored hands of the broken dashboard clock waved Mabel onward, en route to Denver's Children's Hospital. Ann knelt against the backseat, eyes glued to Sarah, who lay motionless.

"Keep talking to me, Sarah. Mom says I need to keep you awake."

■ ■ ■

While Sarah recovered from extensive surgery on her broken arm, Ann found herself sentenced to spending the rest of the summer with Uncle Bob and Aunt Nell, out of her mother's sight. Bob Meyer, Mabel's only sibling, lived with his wife on the old Colorado family homestead, located further northeast as the crow flies.

Initially shaken by the sudden and unexplained upheaval, Ann soon adjusted to the new routine. The ranch grounds—a smattering of sheds and silos, miles of stark white fences, and a massive red barn—had always hollered 'come, explore!'

Although it meant rising early, Ann never missed an opportunity to slip into her red-leather cowgirl boots with their fancy white stitching—a gift from her uncle and aunt to help ease Mabel's sting—and tag along behind her uncle as he wound his way through the maze of corrals during the morning chores.

Soon, though, Ann adhered herself to his side almost exclusively. And since most of her uncle's work days involved extended lunch breaks or early afternoons off, one could find him and his young sidekick anywhere within a thirty-mile radius of the ranch— most often at Mike's Tavern.

Ann felt honored that Mike, the crotchety proprietor with stainless-steel caps on his two upper front teeth, knew to prepare a Shirley Temple for her as soon as he saw Bob's pickup truck through the front window. Each time, a large burger basket followed, overflowing with crispy fries and a full ketchup bottle.

Ann's bi-weekly trek to the bowling alley in the small town of Spearman with Aunt Nell remained equally enticing to her sense of adventure.

Here, playmates appeared like magic, whisking Ann off to the fanciful world of pinball games with their blinking lights and constant clanging.

Once a week, Nell stopped by the small family-owned market on the way home to buy groceries and a special treat for her niece—twisted black licorice ropes, shiny new jacks in a colored vinyl bag, or the latest *Peanuts* comic book.

Ann dubbed Saturday evenings 'Show Night.' Without fail, toe-tapping organ tunes—"Has Anybody Seen My Girl?" the most prevalent—floated through the open living room windows and out into the adjacent cow pasture.

"Thank you!" Ann said one Saturday evening in mid-August as she took her final curtsy. She motioned to Nell at the organ and asked her to stand and take a bow.

Bob cupped his hands around his mouth and shouted. "Bravo!"

At once, Ann unwrapped Nell's dark, velvet-fringed shawl—which she borrowed for each performance—from around her shoulders. She tossed it on the coffee table before landing in her uncle's lap in one giant leap.

"Your turn, Uncle Bob! What're *you* going to do?"

Bob placed Ann on the floor and stood up. "You wait and see, Annie." He grabbed the shawl from the coffee table, draped it over his head, and turned to face the front of the couch. Ann squirmed with excitement as she saw his hand touch the breast pocket of his plaid Western shirt.

With an unrehearsed *ta-da* from the organ, Bob faced his appreciative two-member audience and unfurled the makeshift curtain from over his head.

Aunt and niece exploded with laughter as he winked through the thick black-plastic eyeglass frames hanging from his ears, his dark, thinning hair awry.

Nell watched the bright-red bulbous nose attached to the frames, seemingly interested in knowing if it would keep its shape when he breathed, while Ann rubbed her cheek, imaging how much the wiry-looking black mustache would tickle.

Wiggling a make-believe cigar and donning Groucho Marx's persona, Bob said, "Now, my fine ladies, a few jokes from The Great Roberto! Let us begin! Annie, dear, why did the horse cross the road?"

"Um, I don't know, Uncle Bob!"

"Ah, Annie, I'm not Uncle Bob." In a thick Brooklyn accent, he said, "I am The Great Roberto!"

"Oh, yeah," she replied with a giggle, cheeks shell-pink.

"Okay, ready for the answer?"

"Yes!" they responded in concert.

"Why, my dears, it's because the chicken needed a day off!"

Ann clapped enthusiastically, and another robust *ta-da* escaped from the organ.

"Now, what's the tallest building in the world?"

"I don't know. Do you, Aunt Nell?"

"Can't say as I do, Annie."

Nell twisted her head around and said, "Great Roberto, please tell us the answer."

"The library, of course; it has the most stories, see?"

"Yessiree! That was a good one." Nell laughed, forgetting to strike the keys.

Ann jumped up and down. "Another one, Great Roberto! Please!"

"Yes, one more for you, Annie, my dear. This one's a knock-knock joke. Ready? Knock, knock—"

"Who's there?"

"Anita—"

"Anita, who?"

"Anita hug!"

"Me, too, Great Roberto!" Ann grabbed him around his ample middle and squeezed while Nell played one last *ta-da*.

"Encore, encore! Please, Uncle Bob, one more!"

"Ah, my fine ones, it's time for The Great Roberto to take a break." In one fluid movement, he removed his getup, stashing it back inside his breast pocket.

Nell rose from the organ bench and gave Ann a hug, her long straw-colored locks swaying as she straightened. "All right, Annie, it's time for me to do the supper dishes. You sit out here and keep your uncle company."

"Aunt Nell, before you go, will you please take a picture of me and Uncle Bob? My camera's on the top of the organ."

"Of course." Nell picked up the Instamatic and turned on the flash.

Ann grabbed her uncle's strong, calloused hand and pulled him toward the couch. As they settled back into the russet corduroy cushions—the same reddish-brown shade as the Herefords grazing outside the windows—she maneuvered herself under his arm and snuggled up close against his chest.

She shut her eyes and sniffed his scent of Old Spice.

Bob whispered in Ann's ear. "Let's say chimpanzees when your aunt's ready to snap the picture."

Ann produced a toothy grin. "Okay, Aunt Nell, we're ready!"

"Chimpanzees!"

The flash took. Nell put a hand on one hip. "Talk about a pair of mangy chimpanzees!"

Chuckling, Ann scratched her head and armpits like a cartoon monkey. "Eek, eek!"

Nell set the camera back down on the top of the organ and headed for the kitchen, still laughing.

"Uncle Bob?"

"Yes, Annie."

"I wish you were my dad and Aunt Nell was my mom." She lowered her voice and mumbled. "And I wish I didn't have a little sister. She's Mom's favorite. Sometimes, Sarah makes me so mad, but I promise I didn't break her arm on purpose."

Bob slowly rubbed his forehead, evidently searching for the *right* comeback. "Someday, Annie, when you're older, you'll be glad you have a sister. As for your dad and mom, they both love you in their own special ways."

"But Dad's no fun! He doesn't hang out with me like you do. He's always working and flying off to his company's big office in Boston, wherever that is."

Ann's shoulders dropped, and her voice lowered. "And Mom doesn't like me. She calls me a big brat sometimes, and her face gets red and ugly when she yells at me. And she calls me Turtle in a mean way when she wants me to stand up straight, even though I can't. And now, when I call home, Mom doesn't stay on the phone very long. She's mad at Shorty and me for breaking Sarah's arm. Maybe she hates me."

"Annie, my little chimpanzee, first of all, your dad works hard so he can buy what your family needs. And your mom, she's worried about Sarah's arm getting better and tending to her duties." He smoothed his niece's uneven bangs back with his fingers. "But most importantly, don't blame yourself for Sarah's broken arm. It was an unfortunate accident."

"Okay."

Bob's heart weighed as heavy as iron. "Damn you, Mabel! What's wrong with you?" he said under his breath. He, too, wanted Ann to stay with Nell and him forever. The two of them had discussed it many times.

He leaned over and whispered in Ann's ear.

"You're my favorite girl in the whole world, Annie, my dear. Your aunt and I think you're wonderful just the way you are."

Ann smiled and closed her eyes, Uncle Bob's fierce love settling like silt in the cracks her mother had already chiseled into her heart.

Chapter Four

March 1968

Ann had lost count, certain that a full set of fingers and toes would no longer support the latest tally of questions raised by her younger sister regarding her birth. As she watched Sarah scrutinize the vivid emerald eyes staring back at her in the three-way mirror, Ann braced herself for further inquiries.

"Mommy," Sarah said, pulling on both cheeks until her ghoulish reflection caused her to jump, "are you sure I'm not adopted?"

"Good grief, Sarah; of course, I am. Like I told you the last time you asked, you're the spitting image of your great-uncle Clancy."

Mabel placed her hand on Sarah's head. "He had thick red hair and eyes every bit as green as yours—as *bright* green as ... the pretty leaves on those bushes your father and I planted in the backyard."

"Then, how come you, Daddy, and Annie all have brown hair and brown eyes and no freckles?"

"That's the way God made us, and this is how God made you." Mabel motioned at Sarah's troubled image peering back at them through the dark flecks that appeared like liver spots in the mirror's aged glass. "He did a good job, didn't He?"

"I guess so."

"Certainly, He did!" Mabel set the brush on the vanity and pulled Sarah's hair back into a loose ponytail. Seemingly satisfied, she centered the ponytail on the back of Sarah's head, wrapping it into a tight bun.

Ann sat at the foot of her sister's bed, her bird legs dangling over the low-slung footboard. Then, as certain as day follows night, she turned up the volume on the song snippets playing in her head, muffling the stale chatter once again filling the room.

Instead, she focused on her mother's swift handiwork, longing to receive her own primping. The never-ending realization that a fancy hairdo like Sarah's wouldn't work on her thin, short hair smarted.

"Are we ready, girls?" Fred asked, stepping into Sarah's bedroom.

"Hi, Daddy, how do you like my hair?"

Before Fred could answer, Sarah put on her best Mary Poppins voice. "It's 'supercalifragilisticexpialidocious'! Don't you think?"

"Yes, of course." Fred chuckled. "Hey, let's take a picture for the books."

"You mean *our* picture's going to be in a book?" Sarah asked, eyes big and bright.

"No, that's just an old saying, honey." Fred turned to hide his grin. "Okay, Sarah, you get on your mother's left, and you stand on the other side, Ann Marie. And now, on the count of three, say cheese. Ready? One, two, three."

"Cheeseburger!" the girls said, laughing as they high-fived each other.

Ann and Sarah waited to see the finished Polaroid snapshot.

Fred held the image in his palm long enough for his daughters to watch as the murky blobs developed into three recognizable faces.

"Okay, troops, we'd better hit the road," he urged, ushering Mabel and the girls through the hallway and down the stairs to the back door.

Sarah locked eyes with Ann, eyebrows raised. "Last one to the car's a rotten egg!"

A new '69 blue Chevy Kingswood station wagon had replaced their smaller Rambler station wagon. Mabel insisted on roomy automobiles so that she could haul not only the girls and their paraphernalia but Zeek, too, the family's yellow Labrador mix, a young stray who'd wrangled himself into a lifetime of room and board. She also routinely transported fifty-pound feed bags purchased for the horses, chickens, ducks, rabbits, and barn cats. Fred continued to drive the refurbished '48 Chevy pickup truck that had belonged to his mother and father.

Once seated, the girls cranked down the passenger windows.

"What do you think you're doing, you two?" Mabel asked. "Do you want us all to turn into human popsicles? Roll 'em back up!"

Oh, well. At least she didn't make me and Sarah wear our stupid headscarves! I don't mind wearing the sweater too much.

As they looped around their long driveway and headed west toward Denver, Sarah opened her library book at the tasseled bookmark and read, mouthing the words. Ann halfheartedly picked up on Fred and Mabel's front-seat discussion concerning his upcoming business trip to his firm's Boston headquarters.

She chuckled, envisioning him stuffing his tan leather briefcase with shower caps and other unopened hotel toiletries, along with the miscellany he never failed to bring back for her and Sarah—letterhead stationery and scallop-edged postcards, skinny notepads, and advertising pens.

Even with sparse traffic on West Holt, the thirty-five-minute drive seemed endless to the girls, filled with too many stoplights and flashing pedestrian crossings.

Locating a place to park near the church turned into a difficult situation.

Fred navigated the station wagon into a parking space better suited for a smaller automobile. The stern grimace on Mabel's face as she squeezed out the car door caused him to let out an "Oops!"

"Ann Marie, grab the gift; it's in the grocery bag behind you," Mabel said. "And make sure the card's still attached."

"Okay," Ann replied, suppressing the urge to shake the box. The usual toaster her mother gave would've required a taller box. She noted the card and asked, "What's inside?"

"I know," Sarah answered. "I helped Mommy wrap it. It's a bath towel set ... in a pretty blue color."

"Oh."

That's not very romantic.

"Do you like the shiny silver wedding paper? Mommy let me pick it out and tape on the white bow."

Ann bobbed her head. *Whoop-de-doo, Sarah!*

Before proceeding through the heavy church doors, Mabel instructed Ann and Sarah to straighten their homemade daisy-print sundresses while she removed a stray thread from Fred's jacket. Once inside the narthex, all four family members lowered their voices. Other wedding goers had gathered in small groups. A number of Fred's Rhineholdt Manufacturing associates and their spouses spotted the Castles and waved.

"Hey, Fred and Mabel, over here," Bill Baxter said, motioning.

Fred led the way. The women hugged, exchanging niceties while the men locked hands and exclaimed in jest, "Long time no see!"

"Girls, I'd like to introduce you to a few folks," Fred said.

Sarah shook the extended hands, eyes twinkling when told she had a prizefighter's grip.

Ann sidled up to Mabel and smiled, drawing her hand to her top lip, which she'd wrapped over the edge of her horse-sized buckteeth.

Suddenly, she felt her mother finger the vertebrae between her shoulder blades. As Mabel applied the familiar pressure, Ann jumped to attention, both arms at her sides, her two front teeth exposed.

The painful knuckling dug in deeper—Mabel's tactile warning to pull her shoulders farther back.

Fred's associates smiled back at Ann, but she couldn't see their features through her embarrassment. Her quiet greeting quickly drowned in the adult conversations that resumed. Ann drew her arms across her abdomen, digging her fingernails into the soft, pale flesh of her forearms, oblivious to the deep half-moon impressions left behind.

How come I'm such a stupid, ugly dork? A freaky turtle?

Organ music streamed into the foyer as two young ushers, each dressed in black suits and thin black ties, opened the double doors leading from the sanctuary into the narthex. The random conversations abruptly ended as the ushers led guests down the carpeted center aisle, directing them to either the bride or groom's family's side. Ann recognized the tallest usher—the bride's brother—yet struggled to remember his name. He seemed to recognize her as well and winked.

Pleased but embarrassed, Ann blushed and looked at the floor while Mabel took hold of his arm akimbo. The Castles settled into the next available pew, three rows behind the bride's immediate family.

For years, Fred and Mabel had attended local Rhineholdt functions with the bride, Frances Horton, and her parents, Delilah and Frank—a Rhineholdt machinist.

Those who knew the bride called her Frannie. The Castles had learned that Frannie met the groom last October during their junior year at Colorado University.

Ann sat against the side of the pew along the center aisle while Sarah hopped on Fred's lap, apparently hoping for a bird's-eye view.

Neither Ann nor Sarah had attended a wedding before, so both girls planned on catching every moment. As Frannie made her grand entrance beside her father, fascination placed a chokehold on Ann, an "Oh!" escaping from between her pursed lips.

■ ■ ■

The closest outfit to a wedding ensemble in Ann's collection consisted of Barbie's champagne-colored ball gown, a pair of sparkling gold high heels, and a single-strand pearl necklace with matching stud earrings. Ann squinted as she grasped the second tiny faux-pearl stud and pushed the metal post into the hole in the doll's earlobe.

"There, Barbie, my dear ... no, wait ... I'm going to call you Frannie. Okay, Frannie, you look *posh*!" She giggled, marveling at how easily this new grownup word rolled off her tongue. "And the finishing touch will be your beautiful veil. But listen, young lady," she said, shaking her finger in Barbie's face, "don't you dare let me catch you hunching over in your pretty gown like Ann Marie, the dumb little turtle! Slouching isn't at all becoming. Do you hear me?"

She pinched the doll's head between her thumb and forefinger and rocked it back and forth in a gentle nod. "Good!"

Ann opened the plastic box of straight pins from Mabel's sewing drawer and poked a half-dozen into Barbie's scalp to secure her mesh veil, which several hours ago had held bird seed for the real Frannie's wedding send-off.

She cringed and crinkled up her face.

"Sorry, Frannie! I hope that doesn't hurt too much. Maybe I should've looked for bobby pins in Mom's curler bag instead." She held the Barbie doll at arm's length, adjusted her veil, and said in a dreamy tone, "My! You're even prettier than the real Frannie!"

The Barbie dolls occupied a tall antique pine cabinet painted a shocking blue, a piece of furniture Mabel had acquired at a farm auction years ago.

When the door opened, a three-story, Bohemian-style Barbie pad—designed and executed primarily by Ann—magically appeared. Dazzling colors invited one's hand to reach inside.

The first floor, or bottom shelf, housed Mattel's mod Barbie kitchen.

Miniature color-coordinated utility ware lined the cupboard shelves, and tiny life-like kitchen gadgets overfilled the drawers.

An orange-flowered canister set sat on the countertop next to the plastic sink, and the fully-stocked refrigerator not only looked real, but it also equaled Barbie's height.

Off the kitchen, on the same shelf, stood a cardboard dining table draped with a multicolored fabric piece seized from Mabel's scraps. The table, set for four, held napkins fashioned from light-yellow tissue paper.

A bowl of miniature salt-dough fruit and vegetables that Mabel had crafted with the girls' *help* served as the centerpiece. Empty thread spools had become modern stools.

The living room occupied the next shelf up, and additional *furnished* rooms completed the Barbie cupboard.

The novelty of the cupboard had faded for Sarah.

Her Barbie dolls often sat untouched for weeks on end. For Ann, however, an intended few minutes of play turned into hours of fanciful theatrics.

"Ann Marie, are you still in here?" Mabel asked, opening the door to what she called the rumpus room—a large clutter catch-all with gray cement floors and big picture windows.

"Yes. I'm playing with the Barbie dolls. Come see Frannie! She's getting ready for her wedding!"

Sarah ducked under Mabel's arm and led the way. "Wow, she's a beautiful bride, Annie!"

Before Ann could respond, the smell of fried chicken wafting through the doorway tackled her taste buds. "Mmm, dinner must be ready. Frannie's wedding can wait till later."

Sarah wiped her hands on her plaid apron. "Guess what, Annie! Mommy had me make hushpuppies while frying the chicken. Come try 'em."

Ann flashed a crooked half-smile at her sister, wishing she'd stuck the straight pins into Sarah's head instead of Barbie's. *Why can't Mom stop treating you like her little princess, Sarah?*

Watching her mother and sister interact nauseated her.

"All right, Ann Marie, put the Barbie away," Mabel said in her usual authoritative manner. "You're holding up dinner."

■ ■ ■

By the time Ann had finished her mashed potatoes, she'd decided against resuming Barbie doll play. Instead, she followed Fred from the table and out the back door to the barn. She stood on her tiptoes and dipped the Folgers Coffee can inside the grain barrel until it overflowed with sweet, sticky oats.

She poured an equal amount into Shorty and Rollo's galvanized feed pans while Fred grabbed several flakes from the last bale of Timothy hay.

As her father topped off the water in the trough, Ann took the well-worn curry brush and groomed Shorty's back and hindquarters.

She took great pleasure in watching the pony's shiny dapple-gray undercoat appear as clumps of winter hair fell from the brush.
"Ann Marie, I'm going to put the chickens in for the night. Why don't you finish up?"
"Okay, Dad, I'll only be a few more minutes. Rollo wants his turn."
"See you inside, then." Fred waved his gloved hand and headed for the chicken coop.
Rollo nuzzled Shorty's neck while receiving the same routine. What looked like a powdered sugar dusting of snow soon covered the ground. Ann stooped over and picked up handfuls of the white-and-gray fluff, stuffing it into an empty grain sack before rehanging the curry brush outside the stall. She carried the sack to the front of the barn and tossed it on the top of the rest of the bags Fred would soon be hauling to the dump.
Ann drew her attention upward as she stepped outside the heavy barn door.
Dozens upon dozens of crows had gathered, most alighting on the telephone line overhead, others lining the property fence in the near distance.
She cupped her hands around her mouth and let out her own *caws*, drawing more crows to the ranks. Taking a deep breath, she belted out Aunt Nell's rendition of "Has Anybody Seen My Girl?"
Under the birds' weight, the telephone line dipped into a grin. As Ann skipped backward toward the house, her heart felt light.
Spring had sprung right on course.
"You know what?" Ann said to the crows. "When I walk down the aisle one day, Dad can be on one side and Uncle Bob on the other." A broad grin quickly appeared.
"Yep, that'll look *posh*. And, maybe," she added, fingering the large middle button of her soiled sweater, "Mom will brush my hair and make it look fancy, like Sarah's."

Chapter Five

April 1997

Seldom would Ann crawl into bed to take a nap, yet now, since midmorning, the pesky urge to shut her eyes and power off her mind's chatter kept goading her.

Without bothering to close the blinds or peel off her jeans, she crept under the covers, giving in to the odd little man with his bag of magic sand.

■ ■ ■

Several hours later, the telephone woke Ann. With the grace of a walrus, she pulled herself across Tim's side of the bed, her hand flailing through midair as she reached for the cordless phone. "Hello," she said with a croak, clearing her throat. She sat up cross-legged, placed her hand over the receiver, and let out a yawn.

"May I please speak to Ann Palmer?" asked a pleasant male voice.

Ann closed her gaping mouth. "This is she." Her furrowed brow narrowed. *This better not be a sales spiel, mister!*

"Hello, Ann, my name's Bill Thatcher. Larita Moretti gave me your name as a reference."

Ann's face relaxed.

"Yes, I know Larita well. How may I help you?"

"Well, my wife Selma and I recently moved to the area from

Sacramento. Unfortunately, my 82-year-old mother-in-law, who has terminal cancer, broke her hip several weeks ago. Selma's with her now, overseeing her care at a nursing home outside of Sacramento. Long story short, we've decided to move her out here with us but need someone to help care for her. Larita said she looked after your mother last year."

"Yes, that's correct. And believe me, my mother was a ... shall I say, *character?* But Larita was wonderful with her—the right balance of persistence and tolerance, mixed with ... humor and affection."

The thought of Larita's unending patience produced a sentimental smile. "I used to tease her that her halo grew bigger and brighter every day she was with Mother."

Geez, what a corny thing to say!

She rolled her eyes, frustrated by her admittance to this stranger. "Anyway, Bill, I'm glad you called. I highly recommend Larita."

"Well, Ann, thank you for your candidness. Larita's three out of three on glowing references. We've found our caregiver if she'll have us. I appreciate your time."

"Of course. I'm glad I could help. Best of luck."

"Thank you, Ann. Goodbye, and take good care."

"You, too, Bill. Bye." Ann chuckled as she returned the phone to its cradle, thoughts revisiting her first meeting with Larita.

She propped her pillows against the headboard and leaned back, picking at a speck of lint on her now-disheveled blouse.

My eyes nearly popped out of their sockets the first time I saw Larita.

Who pictures their elderly parent's caregiver as a leather-wearing, Harley-riding, curvy and sexy young woman?

I suppose I was expecting to meet an old, overweight, frumpy lady with broad features and thick-soled shoes. Like someone I'd picture behind the wheel of a run-down station wagon. But not the case with Larita! And speaking of Larita—

Ann hopped off the bed, smoothed back the top sheet and khaki comforter, and set off downstairs to Bernie and Gus' enthusiastic welcome. She shooed them through the kitchen to the back door. "All right, outside with you two." Retracing her steps into the kitchen, she poured a glass of diet soda before retreating to the living room, the afternoon sun streaming through the west-facing windows and turning the dust motes into flecks of sparkling gold.

Ann engaged the drop leaf on the secretary desk.

She picked up the first of a half-dozen new hardback journals laid out on top of its smooth oak surface. The others she placed inside an empty cubby hole.

Careful to set the soda out of the way, she took a seat.

From a manila folder, Ann removed dozens upon dozens of family snapshots tracing back through her childhood and up to the day that Katie had left for college.

A thick stack of handwritten notes—scribbled down after she'd finished sorting through her mother's estate—accompanied the pictures.

These notations remained an integral part of Ann's photo project, the idea of which had transpired from a kitchen-table discussion with Larita nearly one year ago. The accounts would serve as reference points from which she'd write the stories behind her mother's old photos. Not only would the project help to record her family's history, but it'd also be a cathartic exercise aimed at addressing her troubled past.

At first, Ann had balked at the suggestion.

She feared that revisiting events would raise her hackles and that recording them would require too much effort. Soon, though, she'd changed her mind, and with Tim's encouragement, she drove the eighteen miles to Alco in the neighboring town of Silvermile to purchase her first batch of journals.

With an air of pomp and circumstance, Ann picked up her favorite pen and opened the journal to the fly leaf. Across the top, she wrote '1960,' followed by a long, wavy dash, the ending date eventually determined by the last entry.

Seldom, however, did the pen touch the paper as she struggled to develop a rhythm across the lines. By the time Tim arrived home from work, she'd finished placing a period at the end of the sentence on the bottom of page one.

"Hi, Annie," he said, giving her a sideways glance as he took off his windbreaker. "What're you up to, paying bills or something?"

"No, since I've finished the photo albums for Katie and Sarah, I figured I'd start working on the journals." She curled her lip. "It's slow going, though. I look at the earliest photos, when I was three, four, maybe even five, and can't tell if I remember the actual event or just old stories I've heard. And it's possible that I'm filling in the parts I don't remember with a *wee bit* of fiction, you might say." She gestured a small measurement with her fingers.

Tim walked over to the desk and gave her rounded shoulders a squeeze.

"Well, why not start from where you truly remember? How about with first grade at the two-story brick schoolhouse east of Denver? The one with the floodlights above the doorway that reminded you of ... 'bulging frog eyes on the lookout for a meal'?"

"Yeah, Box Elder Elementary School, outside of Aurora in the middle of *the sticks*, with the snakes and the yucca. You remember that picture? Wow! Boring!"

Tim snorted, a smirk plastered across his whiskered mug. "Hey, I do pay attention most of the time!"

"Yep, true statement," Ann said, distracted as she swiped

Wite-Out across the zero in the '1960' she'd written on the journal's flyleaf, replacing it with the number four. She closed the front cover. "Okay, enough for today. Tomorrow, I'll rip out my attempt at the earliest years and start tackling 1964."

Ann caught Tim's glance. "Hey, when the time comes, maybe Aunt Nell will help me out with the earlier facts. Unless she's had it with Mother, her barracuda-of-a-sister-in-law!"

Tim chuckled. "The first time you told me your aunt called her a barracuda, my sides hurt afterward from laughing so hard. Of course, your accompanying theatric routine was the entertaining bit."

"I remember," Ann said, smiling. "But seriously, Mother's never appreciated poor Aunt Nell or maybe even Uncle Bob, for all I know. Her brother. It's sad, isn't it?"

He replied with a nod.

"I hope nothing comes between Sarah and me. If our relationship survived Mother's craziness, it should be strong enough to survive anything."

Ann turned in her seat to face Tim.

"If Sarah and I hadn't grown up in the same household, we probably wouldn't have associated with each other, age difference or not. Sarah's classmates voted her class favorite every year, while mine dubbed me the school's hunchback." She shrank back against the chair.

"And, as you no doubt remember," she resumed, "lapses between her visits home grew longer after she graduated from nursing school. By the time Dad died, and we took over Mother's care, she seldom visited." *Geez, give it a rest! She had to make a living!*

Ann's face softened. "I miss her, Tim. We enjoyed good times together over the years, too. We truly did."

She jumped out of the chair and took Tim's hands in hers. "Oh, my goodness, put the violins away! It's time to shut this pity party down!"

Tim shook his head and smiled his welcome crooked smile, leading Ann through the kitchen toward the back door.

"Why don't we let the dogs inside and head to Del's Diner?" he asked. "No violins there, but we can drop a few coins into the jukebox and see what comes up."

"Great idea! As you may have noticed, I hadn't given dinner a single thought."

As Ann threw on her sweater, the phone rang. "Drat, what's with all the phone calls today? I'd better at least see who's calling." She removed the phone from its cradle and checked the caller ID. "Well, I'll be. It's Sarah, speaking of the devil."

Her face blossomed. "Hello there, sis. How are you?"

"Hey, Annie. I'm fine. I have good news. At least, I hope you think so!"

"Well, I can always use good news. What's up?"

"I'd like to move into Mom and Daddy's old place. There's a great job opening in pediatrics at the hospital in Silvermile. And I could help you on my days off with the photo project you mentioned. It might even be fun. What do you say? I'll pay rent, and we can put the money back into the place. Fix it up. It could be a real win-win situation."

"Of course! That'd be fabulous! When?"

"Would next week be too soon? I just need to line up a U-Haul. I've already started packing."

Ann's face lit up like the Fourth of July. "Name the day, and we'll be there to help unload. Maybe Katie can even break away from classes."

"Okay, I'll let you know when I get the U-Haul business taken care of. It'll be nice to live close to you, Annie."

"It'll be great for us both! I'm excited, Sarah!"
"Okay ... well, talk to you soon. Bye, Annie."
"Bye-bye."

Ann spun around and eyed Tim. "I don't know if you deciphered that or not, but Sarah's moving back to Clifton next week. Into Mother and Dad's old place. Can you believe it?" She pumped her fist. "It's time to put new life into our sisterhood!"

■ ■ ■

As Tim seized the last box from the 20-foot U-Haul truck, this one labeled 'Kitchen: Unbreakable Bakeware' in wide black marker, Ann led Sarah and Katie in a spirited, off-key rendition of "For He's a Jolly Good Fellow."

In no time, however, the trio botched the words and broke into bladder-bursting laughter.

"All right, you hyenas, no more celebrating for you tonight," Tim said, looking over his shoulder before leading the way into Mabel's estate, the door propped open with a cinder block. He set this final box on top of the others, stacked two deep and three high, off to the side of the refrigerator.

Still giggling, Katie pinched the neck of her favorite Ren and Stimpy T-shirt and feigned a deep sniff. "Pee-yeeeuw, Dad, I not only laugh like a hyena, but I smell like one, too ... those raunchy little critters."

"Hyenas or no hyenas ... I don't care what the rest of you think; I get first dibs on a shower," Sarah said, the dark circles under her eyes appearing darker than when she'd first arrived. She freed her long copper mane from the black elastic band and massaged her scalp, her silliness subsiding.

"My muscles are on fire," she continued. "Being back in good old Clifton better be worth all this trouble; moving isn't for lily-livers, that's for sure."

She glimpsed the U-Haul through the kitchen window. "Ugh, listen to me; I'm getting ahead of myself. I better not get too excited till I get the truck and car tow returned." With a thoughtful smile, she added, "And thanks again for all your help, guys."

"Don't mention it, Sarah," Tim replied, waving her off with his gloved hand.

Katie locked elbows with her aunt, dragging her to the front entry. A bright-white grin illuminated her face. "Yeah, Aunt Sarah, you'll get suckered into helping *them* soon, I'm sure!"

Ann came up behind Katie and gave her a playful knee in the backside. "Not without your help, little missy."

"Well, Katie, your mother's already suckered me into helping with her *photo-slash-journal* project," Sarah said, making air quotes with her fingers. "Isn't that right, Annie?"

"Uh, as I recall, Sarah dear, you volunteered. Sucker!" Ann turned toward Katie. "Why don't you and I finish scrubbing the bathroom while your dad and aunt return the truck? And no turning up your nose."

"No, Annie, you two don't need to do that." Sarah draped an arm around Ann's shoulders. "I'm already catching my second wind."

"Nonsense." Ann wiggled loose from her sister's hold and motioned toward the sidewalk. "Now, leave while you still can."

Tim stuffed his gloves into his back pocket and removed his key ring from the front one, holding the Jeep's ignition key out toward Sarah. "I'll drive the U-Haul if you want to take the Cherokee. There's no sense taking your car since it's still packed tight."

Sarah took hold of the key.

Ann and Katie positioned themselves like goofy garden gnomes on the lawn's edge.

"Be back soon," Sarah said. She added with a wink, "But not before you guys are done scrubbing!"

■ ■ ■

Ann handed the framed pencil and charcoal drawing to Sarah.

"Here, for your new kitchen."

"Thanks! You don't want to keep it, huh?"

"No, I still have the real chile ristra. It's more shriveled now, though."

A soft laugh escaped from between Ann's lips.

"Well, I have the perfect spot for it, Annie. And it'll be extra special to me because you drew it."

"You want to hear a story about this drawing?"

"Sure. Go ahead."

"Well, unbeknownst to me, Mother entered a drawing in the Clifton Valley Art Show at the same time as I entered this one."

A broad, mischievous grin captured Ann's lips. "And lo and behold, she received the first-place ribbon while I won second. No biggie, right? At least that's what you'd think."

"Nope, not if Mom was involved."

"Yeah, true. Anyhow, a few weeks later, I stopped by Mother and Dad's to check on them, not realizing that an old co-worker of Dad's was there visiting. And after Dad introduced me, Mother proclaimed to his friend that I'd pouted after receiving second place and refused to acknowledge her first-place ribbon."

"You're such a sore loser!" She held up the drawing and elbowed Ann's arm. "Now it means even more to me, you little meany!"

"Hey, guess what? I've written a few more stories in my journal. In fact, I finished writing about my summer at Uncle Bob and Aunt Nell's ranch. And after finding a Polaroid of Mother, you, and me dressed in our going-to-a-wedding duds, I wrote about Frannie ... I'm blanking on her last name." Ann lifted her shoulders. "Oh, well. It doesn't matter. It's about attending her wedding. And now I'm getting ready to write about the explosion."

"But how about our deep, dark family secret?"

"Yeah, hold onto your hat, sister dear. That's coming. I want everything to be told in chronological order."

"Spoilsport!"

"Hey, the sooner you help me, the sooner I'll get there."

"All right, then. Let's get over to your place and get out those photos!"

Ann bobbed her head. "My sentiments exactly!"

Chapter Six

September – October 1970

Ann lay fully dressed underneath her blue-flowered bedspread, staring vacantly through the sheer canopy, arms folded mummy-style across her chest.

This morning's words ricocheted inside her brain—words spoken in a near whisper yet heard as loudly as if a jetliner had skidded across her scalp.

Drained and confused, she blinked hard, groaning. What could she do to better understand her strange reaction to the small cluster of girls who'd pointed at her, laughing as she entered the auditorium for seventh-grade orientation?

After a time, Ann peeled off the covers and removed her soft leather loafers, tossing them onto the fuzzy bedside rug.

"Maybe this calls for a big fat prayer."

Eyes closed, she sat up cross-legged, lacing her fingers together into a tight ball.

In a hushed and solemn manner, she said, "Hello, God. Do you recognize my voice? It's me, Annie Castle. I'm confused about what happened at school today, and I'm hoping you can help me sort it out."

She bowed her head lower to add greater solemnity.

"It all started when this group of girls talked about me as I walked past 'em in the auditorium. Well, it was the short girl who talked the most." *Short but cute.*

"The girl said, 'Look, *she's* the one Phil used to like.'" *Pointing to me.*

"At first, I was mixed up, but when I saw Terry, my old friend, standing next to the group, I knew she was talking about Phillip Johnston, my third-grade boyfriend."

Ann opened her eyes and looked toward heaven.

"Terry's the one I told you about, God, when I was a third-grader at Dalhart Elementary. He pretended to be a minister and 'married' Phillip and me in Phillip's basement. You remember that, right?" With a soft giggle, she said, "What am I thinking? Of course, you remember because you're God."

She resumed her prayer.

"Then, stupid me, after Terry came over and told me Phillip has a new girlfriend ... probably the short girl ... I got nervous and told him it was fine because I hated Phillip and never wanted to see him again, which is *so* not true—"

A fist rapped on Ann's bedroom door, yanking her back to earth, her eyes landing on her prized horse collection parading across the windowsill. Fred's voice boomed forth. "Ann Marie, I'm leaving for the airport in twenty minutes ... off to Boston. Come downstairs and say goodbye."

"Sure, Dad. I'll be down in a few minutes." With an impatient *humph*, she waited for him to turn and walk back down the hallway.

Before returning to her prayer, she gave her legs a stretch. "Okay, here I go again, God," she said, squeezing her eyelids together tighter than before. "About Terry ... it's weird ... I'm embarrassed for saying such a dumb thing to him—that I hate Phillip—but now... well, now, I'm excited that the short girl called me *she* loud enough for the other girls to hear. I've never thought of myself as a *she* before." *A dumb 'it,' maybe, or ... something inhuman.* Ann opened her eyes once again. "All right, that sounds stupid. It's hard to explain."

Ann lay down on her right side to get more comfortable, pulling her legs to her chest, hands clasping her knees. She drew in a deep breath.

"God, sometimes I feel invisible ... like no one can see me. Not even when I'm standing near them. I'm like a big fat zero, a total nobody."

Um ... a blip on the screen.

"But today, those girls *really* noticed me."

Her chin quivered, tears squeezing past her closed lids.

"I wish people noticed me in a good way like they do Sarah. It makes me mad that they'll never know she kisses Mom's *you know what* so she can get what she wants."

Ann flinched. "Maybe I shouldn't have said that. Sorry, Lord! Now, getting back to feeling invisible. My mom and dad don't seem to see me. What should I do, God? What's so wrong with me?" She sniffled, took off her wire, square-rimmed glasses, and rubbed her sleeve across her damp eyes. *Who am I kidding? Millions of things are wrong with me!*

Especially the way I look.

Nobody has a hunched back like mine. How come I'm the one who has to look like a stupid turtle? A stupid turtle with glasses!

She squeezed her hands tight before letting go. "All right, I guess that's all, God, I ran out of stuff to talk about. Thanks for listening. Amen."

Ann pushed herself upright and slipped her glasses onto her face with one hand. Her eyes immediately landed on the first-day-of-school Polaroid of Sarah and her that sat faceup on the bedside table. She scooted to the edge of the bed and snatched it, bringing it closer for a better look.

The photo depicted the two sisters leaving the house for the school van that morning in new outfits, school bags in hand, looking back at Mabel with big plastic grins. Ann traced her image with her finger, happy to recognize that *she*—this shy, awkward, deformed young girl—had become a real somebody who did belong in this world, even if only an inkling.

Ann's brow creased, and she drew her fingers to her lips, surprised to find herself back in her old fourth-grade Sunday school class.

In her mind, she sat on a kid-sized metal folding chair, listening with a new view on the story of how the lone, crooked sunflower, which the teacher explained "of itself has great value," had become an important part of a beautiful bed of assorted flowers tended to by a kind elderly woman in urban Chicago.

The idea of the lone, crooked sunflower resonated with Ann, yet she longed not to emulate the one in the story.

Yeah, I wanna be a sweet-smelling rose, or a ... pretty purple iris, or ... maybe a daisy. Everybody loves daisies. She shook her head. *How goofy!*

■ ■ ■

Ann played the flute in her junior high's intermediate band and Sarah the French horn in the orchestra at Baldwin Elementary. Both also took private lessons from Mrs. Cotton in Aurora. On weekends, the girls often sat at home on the stiff Spanish-style sofa in front of the bay window, practicing the many simple duets Mrs. Cotton had given them.

"Darn it! Let's start over, okay? I still didn't hit the last note," Ann said, voice raised. She looked at her sister. "Isn't it your turn to start us out this time?"

"Yeah, I guess so." Sarah placed her fingers on the valves. "Okay ... one, two, three, and four."

Together, they played. This time, both girls completed the piece without errors.

"Much better, huh?"

"Yeah, but let's move closer to the lamp, Annie. It's getting dark, and it's hard to see the music."

Sarah propped her horn up against the arm of the couch.

The two sisters grabbed their music stands, placing them in front of the matching wingback chairs facing the couch on the other side of the room.

Ann turned on the brass table lamp between them and sat down.

"Yeah, this is lots better, Sarah," said Ann, planting her feet square with the chair legs, ready to practice once again.

"Hey, Annie, you want to take a break first and get a snack? There's an open box of Girl Scout Cookies on the counter—Thin Mints!"

Before Ann could answer, a thunderous *kaboom* tore through the house—possibly an explosion or a catastrophic weather event.

Fred, upstairs in bed with the flu, barreled down the steps two and three at a time, dressed in cotton boxers and an undershirt.

"Good Lord! Was that a tornado?"

Ann and Sarah—hearts beating hard and fast in their chests—grabbed onto him. Ann screamed, and Fred clapped his hand over her mouth to quiet her.

"Are you hurt?" he asked, grabbing Ann's shoulders with both hands. "Answer me!"

"No!" she said, sobbing.

"Sarah, how about you? Are you okay?"

With a small, shaky voice, she replied, "I'm okay, Daddy."

She pointed to the overturned couch that she and Ann had moved away from minutes ago.

"But look at where the bay window used to be!"

In a hushed voice, Fred replied, "My Lord!"

A gaping hole as large as the station wagon remained where the bay window had been, an unbelievable sight.

Bricks, glass, mortar, and other debris lay strewn across the field in front of the house, hundreds of yards in all directions.

Ann sniffed the air. "I smell smoke! Do you smell it?"

"Girls, where's your mother?"

"She went to the basement earlier to do laundry," Sarah said. She set off running toward the open basement door. A broad plume of swirling gray smoke pushed its way up the steps, out into the hallway.

"Wait, don't you move another inch!"

Sarah froze. Fred took Ann's hand and placed it in Sarah's.

"You both run to the kitchen and call the operator. Tell her to send the fire department to our address. You remember it, don't you?"

"Yes, Daddy, I do," Sarah replied.

"Okay, Sarah, you make the call. Tell the operator that if the fire truck goes under the overpass, it's gone too far. Be sure to remember that part. And after you make the call, you two go outside through the back door and get inside the station wagon."

He bent down. "Your mother and I'll get Zeek out of his pen. Do you understand me? Don't you dare get out of the car, whatever you do!"

Fred's words and tone frightened the girls, but his family's safety had become his sole concern.

He'd put his flu symptoms aside, fear and responsibility driving him forward.

He moved to the top of the basement steps. Clutching the neck of his undershirt, he pulled it over his mouth and nose and felt for the handrail. "Mabel?"

"Fred, I hear you! Don't come down here. I need you to turn off the gas to the house. Did you call the fire department?"

"The girls are in the kitchen now, and Sarah's going to call the operator. I told them to run out and get in the car after Sarah makes the call."

"Good, I'll go outside through the exterior door down here and meet you at the gas tank. We've had an explosion in the crawl space. Thank heavens, the flame's a flicker now, but I'm afraid the basement stairs might be smoldering. A damn fireball sped up the steps and blew the door open."

"Are you okay?"

"My ears are ringing like crazy; otherwise, I'm okay. Now, go, Fred!"

Sarah placed the phone call without faltering. Afterward, the sisters fled to the station wagon, nightfall catching up to them. Once settled, they spotted their parents' silhouettes near the gas tank. Zeek stood between them.

With the gas shut off, Fred returned to the foot of the basement stairway. Little smoke remained. He pulled the pin from the fire extinguisher, pointed the nozzle at the first wooden step, and pulled the trigger.

Soon, the thick white foam saturated the entire stairway.

The girls watched for the fire truck from the station wagon's backend.

The operator had told Sarah that the rig might take up to thirty minutes to reach them this far past the city limits. To temper the wait, they counted the number of cars zipping past their family's long driveway. To the sisters' amazement, not one driver slowed down or seemed to notice the chaos on the top of the hill.

Finally, the fire truck's siren could be heard in the distance, and its red lights grew visible, flashing against the vast tamarind sky.

The girls jumped up and down in their seats, excited that help would soon arrive. But as their father had predicted, the firemen overshot the location, speeding past the driveway.

"Oh, no, Sarah! What should we do?"

"Shut up, Annie! Stop yelling! Why do you always have to be such a stupid baby? The firemen will figure it out and turn around."

The sisters also no longer knew the situation inside the house.

In their parents' opinion, had Sarah given adequate directions on the phone?

And might they be angry with her?

From the house, Mabel also noticed that the fire engine had continued east, missing the driveway. She made her way to the station wagon, Zeek at her heels.

Wasting no time, she slid behind the steering wheel, ignoring Ann's loud whimpers while their Lab jumped into the far back and buddied up to her.

Sarah cringed in her seat, anticipating her mom's annoyance. But like Daddy, she appeared more intent on resolving their troubles.

"Hang on, we're going down the hill," Mabel said, engaging the emergency flashers. She slammed the Chevy into reverse, and—both hands gripping the wheel—she pointed the wagon in the right direction and pressed on the accelerator.

The fireman on the back of the rig spotted the station wagon's emergency flashers and radioed the driver to turn back west. The fire truck soon emerged from underneath the overpass and sped to the Castle's driveway entrance. After spinning the wagon around, Mabel shot back up the hill, leading the way.

■ ■ ■

With the farmhouse condemned by the Aurora Fire Department, the Castles settled into their drab extended-stay room at the Westerner Motorcoach Inn on East Holt—with its two double beds and tiny kitchenette—while major house repairs continued.

Fire investigators had found exposed nails extending down like stalagmites from along the ceiling's four edges in each of the upstairs rooms, revealing that the entire roof had blown straight up and off during the explosion before slamming down into the supporting walls. Mabel resigned herself to the truth that she'd most likely be serving TV dinners this Thanksgiving, although an invitation to Bob and Nell's ranch house remained unanswered. Ann knew it'd be her mother's doing if they didn't spend the holiday with her uncle and aunt and that pleading wouldn't change the outcome. Since the summer Sarah had broken her arm, visits to see them had become fewer.

During this trying time, when not away on a trip to his company's Boston headquarters, Fred left early weekday mornings for the Denver plant, Mabel shuttling the girls to school before heading to the farm for morning chores and to oversee the day's repairs. The nightly farm duties remained Fred's responsibility. After-school routines with Mabel continued without interruption: Monday—4-H; Tuesday—Brownies for Sarah, with Mabel serving her second year as the troop's leader, and Girl Scouts for Ann; Wednesday—church choir practice; Thursday—private music lessons; and Friday—library visit and book returns.

■ ■ ■

Crisp weather prevailed on the last Friday of October.

A stiff breeze carried the remaining dry leaves from the giant elm tree's top branches over the roof of the Aurora Public Library.

Since the library parking lot overflowed with cars, Mabel found a parallel parking space across the street in front of Grover Hardware. "Lock your door, Ann Marie," she said over her shoulder, releasing her lap belt. "And, Sarah, take my hand."

Ann willed herself not to roll her eyes as Sarah obliged, swearing her mother did have eyes in the back of her head, as warned—glowing-red demon eyes.

After double-checking that her door had locked, Ann breathed in the crisp autumn air, enjoying the earthy scent of the trampled leaves. As the three family members reached the main entrance, Sarah dropped her mother's hand, rushing to pull open the glass door for the other library patrons alongside them.

"Thank you, young lady. How kind," said an older gentleman dressed in a plaid overcoat and black felt derby.

Ann cringed as the man patted Sarah on the top of her head with his leather-gloved hand, nodding his approval to Mabel.

"Okay, girls, go your separate ways," said Mabel. "I'll come get you when it's time to leave."

Sarah tapped her mother's arm. "Will you help me find the books about nurses first? I still want to be a nurse and work in a kid's hospital like the one I was in when I broke my arm."

"All right, where do you suppose we should look first?"

"In the subject card file under 'N,' like at school."

"Okay, you lead the way."

Sarah walked over to the long oak file cabinet in the children's section, reciting her ABCs under her breath as she pointed to the correct drawer. "Here it is." She pulled the drawer open and fingered through the tops of the cards.

"Will you help me, Mom?"

Standing beside Sarah, Mabel picked up where she'd left off. "Let's see, there's 'Numb,' 'Number,' and 'Nun.' Ah, here's 'Nurse.'"

Sarah bobbed her head and smiled.

The file card listed five books on nursing. Sarah removed a scrap of paper and a stubby pencil from a small wooden box on the top of the card file, jotting down the Dewey Decimal information for the two Florence Nightingale biographies. Mabel watched as Sarah squatted on one knee and located them on a bottom shelf.

"Found 'em! Thank you, Mom," Sarah said, walking toward a bright-yellow beanbag chair situated by the big picture window overlooking the yard.

Mabel located Ann in the teen area before she wandered over to the travel section.

For years, she had been threatening to book Fred a one-way flight to *Timbuktu* if he didn't concede to a tropical trip for the two of them. Since the explosion, however, the family would need to get settled back into the house first.

And that seemed more than enough for Mabel—to be back in their home with the explosion worries behind them.

Books on exotic places to visit would substitute for now.

With three books in hand—two on general horse care and Western riding techniques and the third a compilation of short stories about farm life—Ann located an empty seat at a table near the book checkout.

Mabel stood next in the line at the counter. Ann motioned to her but failed to get her attention.

"Hello, Mrs. Castle, how are you today? Did you find what you needed?" asked the elderly Mrs. Gravitz, who knew both mother and daughters by name yet presumably had no knowledge of their house explosion outside the Aurora city limits.

"Yes, thank you, I did. These two Hawaii travel guides will do."

Mabel set both books on the countertop. "It looks like you're busy this afternoon. The change in weather must be driving everyone inside."

"Yes, I believe so," the librarian replied, stamping the return due date on the inside jacket cover. "Sarah showed me a picture of Florence Nightingale. Says she's going to be a nurse when she grows up."

"Well, she has the brains and moxie for it," Mabel said, nose in the air. "Sarah could achieve anything she wants."

She leaned in closer to Mrs. Gravitz and lowered her voice.

"Her sister, on the other hand, doesn't have what it takes to be a professional of any sort. Ann Marie's not what I'd call ... *successful material*. Her tank's half-full compared to Sarah's, should I say? Ugh!" She shrugged, lip curled.

"And she'd never look like a professional with her hunched back," she continued. "I often say Ann Marie looks more like a turtle!"

How could any mother speak like that about her daughter to a virtual stranger in a public place, especially without provocation? And what if the young girl could hear?

The kind librarian nodded and made the suitable *mm-hmm* sounds but offered no comments to Mabel's negative appraisal of Ann. Instead, she cast a sympathetic glance at the girl.

Ann sat at the table, engrossed in her books, treating them like prized possessions. Occasionally, she rubbed their covers and sniffed their sweet, musty smell.

She looked so attentive and focused on her reading that it seemed far-fetched and unfair to say she *wasn't all there*. Why couldn't she become anything and anyone she wanted? She seemed eager to learn.

Not surprisingly, Mabel appeared unrattled by the lack of response from her one-woman audience.

And she still had more to say regarding her awkward, dimwitted eldest daughter. Her voice grew louder.

"Believe me, I do my duty by ordering her to pull her shoulders back, but she refuses to cooperate. She'd rather embarrass me by looking like a hunched turtle. If only I could swap her for another Sarah." Her tone sharpened. "No respectable profession would hire Ann Marie! I tell you, she's not *successful material*!"

Ann flinched upon hearing the tail end of her mother's rant. Hands trembling, she closed her book and moved across the wide room.

I'll never be as good as that brat Sarah or anybody else, for that matter!

Too many things are wrong with me. Too bad I didn't get blown to bits in the explosion. Huh, Mother? Too bad I didn't die like you want me to.

Through large tears, Ann dug her fingernails into her forearm, hoping to draw blood.

Chapter Seven

April 1971

A smattering of new homes, most on ten-acre lots, stood willy-nilly across once-open farmlands and brought young families to the prairie east of Aurora. Ann and Sarah delighted in the fact that a bonafide school bus had replaced the worn-out commercial van that had always transported them to and from school.

Ann often spent her Saturday afternoons in the company of a few of these new neighbors, but not before taking a stab at her self-imposed cleaning chores, which varied weekly and included the kinds of messes that made her squirm: the gritty dust bunnies cowering in the corners, the wads of tissues and chunks of dried-out foods still sitting where they'd dropped, and the spattered toothpaste freckles coating the bathroom basins.

All of these messes accorded well with the toppled stacks of this and the uneven mounds of that scattered throughout the house.

Once Ann deemed her surroundings tolerable, she lined up a playmate, preferably fellow classmate Sammy Spellman who lived a couple of miles to the southeast.

Lucky—a five-year-old sorrel quarter horse gelding—had become Ann's favorite mode of transportation to and from those visits. He beat out her Sting-Ray bicycle by a broad margin, even with its sky-blue frame, ape handlebars, and metallic banana seat.

Hand-picked by her uncle Bob, Lucky had joined the two ponies, Shorty and Rollo, on Ann's "Lucky 13th Birthday" last fall, several weeks before the family returned home from the Westerner Motorcoach Inn following the explosion.

A heartwarming card had come with him:

Dear Annie,

We're <u>lucky</u> to have such a special niece as you, so <u>lucky</u>, in fact, that this fine fellow shall be known as <u>Lucky</u> from this day forward. May you two share many happy miles as you make many happy memories.
Happy <u>Lucky</u> 13th!

XOXO,
Aunt Nell & Uncle Bob

Ann swore a better confidant couldn't be found in a human being.

She shared both her troubles and joys with Lucky—from Phillip's constant avoidance of her at school to making first-chair flute before the spring concert, even though her frequent shaking from nervousness caused too much vibrato and made the other kids laugh more often than not.

■ ■ ■

The Saturday after Easter brought short-sleeve weather for the first time that spring. Fred and Mabel worked outside, putting in new raised garden boxes before Fred departed for Boston on Sunday night's red-eye flight.

Sarah sat cross-legged atop the mound of fresh topsoil, making squiggly designs with a twig while waiting for her friend Melissa's mother to drop Melissa off for the afternoon. All three turned toward Ann and Lucky when they heard the *clip-clop* of horse hooves behind them.

"Hey, where are you off to, Ann Marie?" Fred asked, wiping his sweaty brow across the sleeve of his T-shirt.

"Haha, Dad! You know where I'm going! I asked you if I could go over to Sammy's house when she returned my call fifteen minutes ago!"

Fred winked. "Very well, then."

"Did you and your father set a time for you to be home?" Mabel asked. She removed her wide-brimmed straw hat and used it to fan her face.

"Yes, five o'clock. We even synchronized our watches. Right, Dad?"

"That's how I remember it, Ann Marie," he replied with another wink.

Mabel's brow puckered. "All right. But I'm warning you, you better keep a close eye on your watch."

Ann dipped her head in compliance, her smile disappearing at her mother's stern tone. *Mom, you even take away the sun's glow! At least you do in my universe!*

"Hey, before you go, Annie, can I take a picture of you and Lucky with my new camera? *Can* I?" asked Sarah.

"It's *may* I, Sarah. You know that," Mabel said with a gentle scolding. Her tone with Sarah never sounded scathing, merely instructional—nothing like when she'd speak to Ann.

Sarah smiled and nodded at her mother before turning her attention back to her sister.

"Sure, you *may*, Sarah." Ann rolled her eyes, careful to avoid Mabel's sightline. "But hurry! Please! Sammy's gonna walk in this direction to meet me."

"Okay, my camera's right inside the back door."

Sarah jumped up, dusting off her pink polka-dot shorts, Zeek hot on her heels.

Ann had decided to ride bareback so she, too, could wear shorts. If Sammy had permission to get out the dirt bikes, she figured she could borrow a pair of jeans since Sammy's dad, a stickler for the rules, never allowed anyone to ride with bare legs.

"See! Here it is!" Sarah said, holding up her Instamatic from the back door.

"Good, that was fast." Ann stretched forward. "Okay, Lucky. I'll put my arms around your neck."

"Yeah, that looks great." Sarah peered through the viewfinder and clicked her tongue. "Look over here, Lucky!"

Ann smiled wide. "Cheese Whiz!"

"Got it!" Sarah advanced the film and slipped her wrist through the nylon wrist strap, leaving the camera to dangle like a charm.

Reining Lucky toward the driveway, Ann waved. "See ya guys later."

■ ■ ■

Sammy hadn't traveled far from her house. She stood alongside the road, munching on something.

Ann cupped her hands around her mouth and shouted. "Hey, Sammy! What's up with you? What're you eating?"

"Here, catch!" Sammy tossed an apple too wide to the right.

Ann hopped down, leading Lucky by the reins. The soft earth of the newly plowed field filled her tennis shoes. "Geez, thanks for throwing it in the dirt!" Before biting into the apple, she wiped it off on her good T-shirt—the one with the black *peace* sign. She knew the pulp would stick to her braces, yet she couldn't resist the enticement.

"Sorry! No wonder nobody asks me to be pitcher." Sammy tossed her core in the ditch and wiped her hands on her jeans.

"Wanna ride? I'll give you a leg up," Ann said.

"Sure. Why not?"

Ann chuckled to herself as she recalled the last time Sammy had ridden Lucky bareback. It took place in the corral behind the barn on a warm fall day right after she'd received him from her uncle and aunt. The two rode double, Sammy in front.

As the ride ended and Ann dismounted, her hand caught in the loop of Sammy's halter top bow, untying it and leaving her fully exposed.

Ann stood still, mortified, until Sammy rocked back and forth, howling with laughter.

Then, unable to stop laughing, Sammy wet her pants—dusty rivulets flowing between Lucky's hooves. Not missing a beat, she jumped down, crawling into the horse trough to rinse off.

"Yoo-hoo, Annie! Are you in outer space? Aren't you coming aboard?"

"Uh ... no, I'll walk," Ann replied with a soft chuckle.

"You silly girl!"

Hank, Sammy's little brother, spotted the girls through the front window and came charging outside. "Can I ride Lucky? Can I, huh, Annie? Pretty please with a cherry on top?"

Ann quietly laughed. *Good thing my mother's not here, Hank. She'd have 'canned' your 'can' in an instant!*

Annoyed by Hank's questions, Sammy jumped down and answered her baby brother before Ann could speak. "Once around the house, and that's it. Got it, bud?"

"Okay! Wahoo!" Hank turned around in celebratory circles.

The girls helped him up and had him grab a fistful of mane with both hands.

Ann took the reins, and Sammy walked alongside. Hank talked sweetly to Lucky, seemingly glad to tune out all else.

"All right, we're done, Hank," Ann finally said. "You even received an extra trip around the house."

Sammy pulled him off Lucky's bare back.

"Thank you, Lucky and Annie!"

"Hey, Hank, aren't you going to thank me, too?" Sammy asked, tone snide.

"Thank you, Sammy!" he answered with a big, cheesy grin. He looked at Ann. "Can I kiss Lucky on the forehead?"

"That's ridiculous!" Sammy said, rolling her eyes.

Ann pulled Lucky's head down. "On the contrary, he'd like that, Hank!"

Sammy stomped the bare ground, hands flailing through the air. "Ugh! Ann Marie Castle, I'm supposed to be the one in charge of Hank!"

Ann ignored her outburst, tying Lucky to a section of fence shaded by the low sloping garage roof.

The next few hours held all types of activities: troll doll play—even though the girls believed themselves too mature and *pinky swore* not to tell anyone; a sneak sip of cold coffee and a few sucks on a cigarette butt that Sammy's parents had left at the kitchen table; and an episode of *Mr. Ed* with Hank, prompting the girls to teach Lucky to wiggle his lips, too, using a chicken feather and a long stick.

The friends even made a botched attempt at mimicking a trendy hairdo that turned into a definite *hair-don't*. The two schoolmates dove into everything but the dirt bikes. All the while, Ann periodically peeked at her wristwatch, careful to allow twenty minutes to make the trek home.

Finally, after their game of War ended in a tie, the girls decided to postpone the tiebreaker until the next school bus ride or available Saturday afternoon. Sammy put the dog-eared card deck back inside the cupboard and walked Ann to the door.

"Need a boost?" Sammy asked.

"No, thanks anyway; I can jump up on your dad's sawhorse and get on from there."

As Ann wielded Lucky toward the roadway, Mabel came barreling up to the edge of the driveway in the station wagon. A thick cloud of dust erased the rubber-wheeled brute from sight as she brought it to a screeching halt. When the air cleared, Ann eyeballed an elm tree branch, its young leaves poking out the open passenger window. *What the heck?*

Mabel leaned over and grabbed the branch. She jumped out of the door and shook it at Ann, causing Lucky to spook.

"Ann Marie, get over here right this minute with that horse!"

"But, Mom!" she said, allowing the words to slip from her tongue before she could catch them. "What did I do wrong? I was *heading* home. It's only four-thirty."

"I don't want to hear one more peep out of your mouth, young lady!" Mabel flung the spanking switch into the barrow ditch. "Here, give me those reins!"

Ann obeyed. Mabel yanked horse and rider around to the driver's side, feeding the reins through the window. She turned the key in the ignition, backed out onto the roadway, and straightened the wheel. Slowly, Mabel rolled along toward home, daughter and mount in tow. Ann glanced back at Sammy's house, hoping she and Hank hadn't witnessed this degrading two-man parade.

Once home, Ann gave Lucky a quick rubdown and put him away in his stall before going upstairs to her bedroom. Here, she sat in silence and reflected upon her 'wrongdoing' as instructed. After the rest of the family had finished dinner, Mabel ordered her back downstairs to fix herself a plate from their leftovers.

"And don't forget to clean up the kitchen," her mother said in a steely tone as Ann passed through the living room. Mabel's hawk-like stare from her perch on the sofa caused Ann to move in double time.

Although tempted by the smell of the macaroni and cheese, Ann's appetite had all but disappeared.

After eating only a few bites, she covered the casserole dish with Saran Wrap and put it in the refrigerator. In slow motion, she rinsed off her family's dinnerware, individually placing each piece into the dishwasher, her mind rehashing the day's debacle.

This isn't fair! I didn't do anything wrong. Sammy's mom would never do this to her. I should run away, Lucky and me. Bet we could make it to Uncle Bob and Aunt Nell's.

Ann crinkled her face.

But they'd probably rat on me and say it was for my own good. This sucks! Mom—no, change that to Mother—is such a witch ... no ... a bitch!

I'm never going to call her Mom again! It's 'Mother' from here on out!

Sarah had forgotten to take off her apron and snuck into the kitchen, tapping her sister on the shoulder. "Psst. Hey there."

Ann jumped, whacking her shin on the edge of the dishwasher. In a whisper, she said, "Geez, Sarah, what'd you do that for? You scared me to death." She rubbed her shin before wiping her hands on the soiled dishtowel. "So, do you know why Mom's ... oops, I mean *Mother's* mad at me? I can't figure out what I did wrong unless it's because I wore my good shirt today."

"No, I'm pretty sure it wasn't your shirt. After Melissa's mom picked her up, Mom told Daddy that you were supposed to be home by four-thirty. When she didn't see you coming up the driveway, she slammed out the door and tore a branch off the tree."

"I swear, Dad and I agreed I didn't have to be home until five o'clock. What did Dad say to her?"

"That he'd told you five o'clock, but then he said maybe he didn't." Sarah took off her apron, doubled it up, and tossed it in the linen drawer. Looking at her sandaled feet, she added, "I better go before I get in trouble, too."

Ha, Sarah! You getting into trouble's a big fat joke.

■ ■ ■

The screen door snapped shut even though Fred tried to close it gently.

Ann's bedside clock read ten-thirty, time for her dad to leave for the airport to catch Sunday night's red-eye flight.

Mabel thumbed through an assortment of women's magazines stacked beside her on the full-size bed, which she no longer shared with Fred. Rather, her hot water bottle had become her new bedmate. She routinely used it to soothe her 'tense muscles,' providing comfort.

Tonight, though, Sarah's rhythmic breathing, audible through the open bedroom door next to hers, had presumably become her sole comfort.

Darn it! Why can't I fall asleep as fast as Sarah? Curled up in the fetal position, Ann attempted to relax *her* muscles—starting with her forehead—while counting backward from fifty. Nonetheless, sleep still evaded her. Next, she slid onto her back with her extra pillow tucked under her calves. Agitated when that failed, she finally turned from her left side, legs at right angles, to her right side, feet flexed.

Nothing worked. Instead, Ann lay on her stomach and reached under the mattress for her diary, the one with the lock and key and the skinny, blue-flowered matching pen that Sammy had given her.

Afraid Mabel might notice if she turned on her lamp, Ann probed around in the top drawer of her bedside table for her flashlight. "Bingo!"

She opened the diary, placing the key in the bowl-shaped base of the hobnail lamp for safekeeping. Taking the pen in hand, she closed her eyes and created an outline in her mind. *Okay, here I go!*

The diary—a new means by which to catch God's attention—had replaced her intimate conversations with Him.

Sunday, April 18th

Dear Diary,

Sorry I didn't write yesterday, but it was such a WEIRDO of a day! Thank goodness today was lots better! I had Sunday school at ten o'clock with Mrs. Feldman, and I attended church with Mom, Dad, and Sarah an hour later. After the service, we ate brunch at the pancake house by the fire station. I had my usual blueberry pancakes drowning in syrup and whipped cream, with hash browns on the side.

As we were leaving, this little girl threw up on the restaurant floor.

It almost hit my dad's shoes. It was GROSS! It makes me feel like throwing up just thinking about it! Yuck, I can still smell it!

I wish I could fall asleep now. Then wouldn't it be COOL if a big fat pink eraser appeared in my dream and erased all the ugly parts of yesterday out of my mind for good?

> That way, I'd only be able to remember the fun I had with Sammy. Hank, too, but I'd never admit that to Sammy! He's pretty sweet for a little kid. I bet Sammy only pretends that he drives her nuts!
> Well, at least I didn't get whacked with the branch this time! It would've hurt on my bare legs. But being grounded for a whole month is way too long!
> And it also bothers me that Dad didn't stick up for me. You know, Dear Diary, sometimes I wish Sarah was a boy instead of a girl. Everything with Mom is about Sarah. Maybe, if I had a little brother instead of my sister, she wouldn't compare me to him. I know things aren't always Sarah's fault, but sometimes, I can't stand either of them. I'm sorry for feeling that way (and for sucking on the cigarette butt yesterday)! I hope God still lets me into Heaven when I die! Goodnight.
>
> Your friend,
> Annie Castle

Chapter Eight

May 1997

The fragrant late-spring air wrapped itself around Ann's body like a sheer scarf. She stood on the front porch, thirsty to drink it in.

To the near west, Mt. Polk had suited up in this season's luscious green shades. And to the east, the foothills, slathered in brilliant morning sunlight, flaunted their cloaks of mammoth boulders and pinon pines.

Overhead, Canadian geese seemingly honked in gratitude for clear skies.

"Couldn't ask for a nicer day, huh, fellas?" Ann said to Bernie and Gus, who nearly knocked her off her feet as they dashed down the porch steps and into the driveway. Gus let out a thunderous yowl. "Geez, what's up with you two?" She jerked around to see a white older-bodied car pull into the driveway. Clapping repeatedly, she called the dogs. "Bernie, Gus, come here!"

The car came to an abrupt stop, not ten feet from where Ann stood.

She caught herself squinting through the windshield at a middle-aged woman with big hair and oversized sunglasses.

Unable to place her, Ann looked at the ground, her cheeks turning brake-light red.

"For crying out loud, Annie," the female voice said from the open driver's side window, "don't you recognize an old high school chum when you see one? Maybe you need to clean your glasses!"

Ann trotted around to the open window. "Yvonne, is that you? Oh, my gosh, it's good to see you! How *long* has it been?"

Accompanied by the snap of her Juicy Fruit gum, the door groaned open, and Yvonne stepped out, heavier than when Ann had last seen her but still a character.

Dressed in a vibrant flowered tank top and a pair of last decade's billowy parachute pants, Yvonne wrapped her arms around her old friend, rocking her back and forth with the strength of a wrestler.

Ann dug her feet into the gravel to keep from falling.

"We haven't seen each other since Katie's birth!" she replied, voice pinched.

Yvonne let go and took a small step backward to catch her breath.

"I'm afraid so, Annie. Hard to believe it's so easy for best buddies to lose touch. Glad you're still living in this same house so I could easily find you. Anyway, that aside," she said, dancing on tiptoes, "I'm moving back here to Clifton! Brady, you remember him, don't you?"

Yvonne snapped her gum. "He and I were dating when you were pregnant." She placed her hand on Ann's shoulder. "Oh, yeah, by the way, I'm glad Katie recovered so fast from that lung *thingy* … you know, the breathing problem she had after she was born. What was it called?"

"Hyaline membrane disease." With a firm nod, Ann said, "Yep, she'll be a junior in college this fall and is no worse for wear."

She patted Yvonne's hand.

"And, yes, I remember Brady. Tall and skinny. Dark hair. Nice looking guy."

"Well, not so skinny anymore." Yvonne pinched her tubby middle. "He's packed on even more weight than I have. Anyway, we divorced a year ago, and now, here I am, looking for a fresh start. At least we didn't have any kids, thank goodness." She removed her sunglasses and pointed to Ann's Jeep.

"Please don't tell me you're going somewhere. I'd like to catch up on each other's lives, Annie." With a downcast glance and another loud snap of her gum, she added, "But I can come back later."

"Nonsense, my errands can wait."

Ann took hold of Yvonne's forearm. "The day's all ours. Come on."

The two friends locked elbows and said, "Can you dig it?"

Yvonne laughed deep from her belly. "My Lord! Can you believe we used to say that in high school and thought we were cool? We were pathetic!"

"Go figure," Ann replied with a throaty chuckle.

The dogs slipped inside the house first.

Yvonne held out a hand as Gus and Bernie took a friendly sniff and reveled in a few pats. "Hi there, guys." She straightened, brushing her hand across her pants. "I'm gonna have to make a trip to the pound as soon as I get settled. But first things first." She spun around on her heels.

"I wanna stand here and check out your living room. You've always had a knack for taking ordinary things and giving them *oomph*! Like your collection of mismatched silver candlesticks on the top of the desk. If I did something like that, it'd look awful."

Ann waved her off. "Baloney."

She pointed to the couch. "Have a seat and make yourself comfortable. Is diet soda okay? Or I can put on a pot of coffee? Although decaf might be all there is."

"Nope, no soda or coffee, Annie, my friend. This calls for

something stronger! And I happen to have the *right* something in the car. Crack out the wine glasses, would you, please?"

Ann glanced at her wristwatch. "Ugh...it's ten-thirty in the morning! Isn't it too early for wine?"

Yvonne put on a crooked smirk. "We won't make it a habit. Okay?"

"Well, it's not like Mommy dearest can take a switch to my backside anymore," Ann replied, replicating her old friend's sly smile.

By the time Yvonne returned with the Riesling, Ann had pieced together a small platter of crackers, cheese slices, and juicy green grapes and placed it on the steamer-trunk-turned-coffee-table along with two wine glasses.

Yvonne poured a generous amount into each glass and offered up a toast. "To a renewed friendship. May it blossom once again!"

"Definitely," answered Ann, tapping Yvonne's glass and taking a sip.

After a hefty gulp, Yvonne rolled up her stale gum in her napkin and made a three-tier cracker and cheese sandwich, taking a bite. "Now, Annie, I remember what a lightweight drinker you used to be."

"Still am! It only takes one margarita at Little Lolita's."

"My point exactly. So before you get all nonsensical and chatter away like a magpie, please catch me up on your life, would you?"

Ann kicked off her clogs and settled back into the leather cushion, tucking her feet underneath her. "What do you want to know first?"

"Well, are your parents still living?"

"No, Dad passed away from melanoma in '94, and Mother died a year later, following hip surgery and a long struggle with emphysema. It was weird, though—" Ann's forehead wadded up. "When Dad was terminal, and hospice had been called in, Mother retreated to the other end of the house for weeks on end. It was like she'd disappeared off the face of the earth."

Not that her disappearance wouldn't have caused rejoicing. Okay, that's not nice.

"For heaven's sake, why would she do something like that?"

"Sarah and I figured she was jealous of the attention Dad was getting."

Ann shrugged. "But I don't know. Maybe that wasn't the case. Mother never would say." She took another sip. "Remember the time at the beginning of our sophomore year when we were riding around with Betz and the other girls in her brother's Mustang, and I was worried about her getting me home on time? I knew Mother would clobber me if she didn't."

Yvonne nodded, face glum.

"Yep, it was the evening before the regional championship football game. Betz stopped by the town park and left us stranded while she and the other two girls ran off to talk to somebody else."

"Yeah, and by the time I made it home from the park, I was late. I still remember the huge welts on the backs of my thighs from the cottonwood branch Mother kept whacking me with. But the worst part, by far, was having Betz and the rest of you drive by and see her beating me in the driveway."

Yvonne grimaced. "Tell me, did your relationship with your mom get better?"

Ann's eyes grew large. "Wow! You don't know about the big family secret I uncovered, do you?"

"What secret?"

"Okay, let's backtrack. I'll start with Larita."

"Who's Larita?" Yvonne asked, fingering a grape. "I don't remember anyone named Larita from high school."

"That's because Larita's from Denver. She was Mother's caregiver ... a godsend ... my hero. I used to tell her that her halo grew brighter every day she spent with the old hen. I swear the tension between Mother and me was unbearable toward the end of her life. I couldn't even stand to touch her." Ann's body drooped. "Whoa, that's hard to admit out loud, yet it was true."

Yvonne reached over and rubbed Ann's forearm.

"That's understandable, Annie. You have no reason to feel bad about your feelings. A feeling isn't right or wrong; it's your heart's way of talking to you."

Ann placed her hand on top of Yvonne's. "Thanks, my friend. Larita said nearly the same thing. In fact, hang on. I'll be right back. I want to show you something."

"Okay, Annie. I'm not going anywhere."

Yvonne made another cracker sandwich and took a bite.

Upstairs, Ann knelt in front of the espresso-colored nightstand and removed a handful of journals from its cubby. She slid her fingers down their glossy spines, amazed by the number of family tales penned across their plain parchment—some amusing and endearing, many mundane and predictable, and others teetering on the fringe like nearly spoiled fruit. She pushed herself upright off the thick sisal rug and swiped at the imprints left behind at the knees of her jeans.

"I'd like to show you these journals," Ann said, holding them up as she entered the living room. She sat down once again, the journals in her lap. "I have to give Mother credit for taking lots of pictures over the years."

She rolled her eyes and snorted.

"Of course, she never put them into any semblance of order or kept them in one place. I found photos inside envelopes, books, drawers, and even purses while sorting through the estate! Anyway, long story short, Larita came up with the idea that I jot down the stories behind the pictures ... a subtle form of therapy. And that's what's written inside these journals."

"Has it helped? Writing the stories?"

"Yes, I believe it has. I ... know deep down that Mother did the best she could at the time."

Ann thumbed through the top journal.

"And I do believe she was mentally ill. Sadly, she never saw it, I guess. She never sought help anyway. Maybe it was too much of a stigma—given her generation, I mean. At any rate, I've mourned, if you will, what never was."

"I don't catch what you mean, Annie."

"I mean never having a genuine mother-daughter relationship. Never talking about my future and boys, sharing secrets, or having a soda or a cup of coffee together—simple, everyday things. Talking, period, the way most girls do with their moms."

She shrugged, raising her hands. "I mainly remember being ignored. But if not that, I was being shamed about my hunched back."

Ann held up a finger.

"And it was my back that was truly the bane of her existence. Remember me telling you how she'd dig her fingertips hard into my vertebrae and call me Turtle?"

Ann prodded her forearm, emulating her mother's cruel, jabbing style.

Yvonne's eyes widened.

"She kept that up well into my high school years. She'd even do it discretely in public. It used to embarrass the crap out of me."

Noticing Ann's tears, Yvonne handed her an extra napkin before taking hold of her hand.

"I remember feeling bad for you, Annie, and thankful that she wasn't my mom." Yvonne shot up in her seat. "Okay, I want to hear about this big family secret!"

A soft laugh escaped Ann's mouth. "All right, I'll see if I can give it to you in a nutshell ... well, maybe a giant conch shell." She held out her wine glass. "Better fill it to the rim!"

Chapter Nine

April 1972

Several hundred yards to the west of the barn stood Mabel's pet project for the past decade—the newly renovated 1920s Willow Creek Schoolhouse, once a one-room site for instruction in 'the three R's' for first through eighth-graders in early rural Aurora.

Ann remembered little of the short ride to the schoolhouse's original location, where her mother had purchased it for a pittance, along with two dilapidated one-hole outhouses, a thirty-foot flagpole, and an assortment of broken-down playground equipment.

Neither did she clearly recall watching Mabel's acquisition arrive at the farm less than a month later aboard a trio of flatbed trucks—"piggyback," as Fred had called it—new concrete foundations awaiting its arrival. Nor did Ann fully recollect playing the role of 'Daddy's little helper' as he repaired the merry-go-round, swing set, and wobbly teeter-totters.

Now, years later, past the narrow entryway where schoolchildren had once hung their coats and stowed their lunch tins, six rows of five vintage wooden school desks in graduated sizes sat atop the marred hardwood floor.

Every desktop held a glass inkwell and a horizontal indentation for fountain pens and graphite pencils. Carved initials appeared in inconspicuous spots in the soft wood, and petrified chewing gum remained on the bottoms of random desktops and seats.

Behind the teacher's desk, above the wainscoting, hung two

large green slate chalkboards. Here, Mabel had written a sampling of unsolved arithmetic problems.

A Ben Franklin wood-burning stove took up the northwest corner, while at the opposite end of the room, on the top of a rickety wooden stool, sat Mabel's mock-up of a *dunce hat*—a stiff costume witch hat from which she'd cut away the brim and hand-painted the word 'DUNCE' in large white capital letters.

On the wall above the stool hung an antique wooden spanking paddle, loosely referred to as the 'board of education.'

Not surprisingly, the visiting Aurora fifth and sixth graders voted the dunce corner their favorite part of their field-trip experience to the old schoolhouse.

■ ■ ■

Sarah's sixth-grade class became the first attendees to what Mabel had deemed on the homemade flyers as *A Day at the Old Country Schoolhouse.*

Twenty-one bright shining faces filled the student desks.

"Say 'Yankee Doodle Dandy,'" Mabel said, snapping a picture of the class with her Polaroid camera. Most of the pupils had dressed in period-style garb and hairdos while Miss Mannis, her long locks twisted in a talcum-powdered bun, looked the part of a *schoolmarm*. Clothed in a dark floor-length skirt, crisp white blouse, and black fringed shawl, she presided over her class, teaching from the period readers and textbooks Mabel had supplied.

The unpredictable springtime weather proceeded to cooperate into the noontime hour.

A sack lunch picnic unfurled across the playground as Lucky and the ponies craned their necks over the corral fence to watch.

Mabel helped Miss Mannis dole out cups of ice-cold lemonade

she'd hand-squeezed before dawn and a selection of cupcakes and cookies that several of the students' mothers had provided. Bathroom breaks took place in the house instead of in the two outhouses, much to the boys' disappointment.

At two o'clock, Miss Mannis pulled out the antique brass school bell from the bottom desk drawer. Its clinging sound rang sharp and clear. "Sarah, will you please escort your mother to the front of the room?"

Applause erupted as the children jumped to their feet.

"Mrs. Castle," continued Miss Mannis, "thank you for the privilege of being the first class to experience a day of learning in your remarkable one-room schoolhouse. It's an experience we won't soon forget." She looked at Sarah and motioned for her to proceed with the presentation of her mother's gift.

Sarah flashed a star-studded smile and slid a large planter of springtime annuals across the teacher's desk to where her mother stood. "Mom, this is for you from all of us." A clever thank you card cut from white construction paper in the shape of the school building and signed by each student accompanied the gift.

"What a terrific surprise! Thank you, everyone. I'm pleased that you enjoyed your day at the Willow Creek Schoolhouse." Mabel concluded the field trip by having the children line up around the flagpole for a short flag-lowering ceremony.

Before the children boarded the school bus bound for Baldwin Elementary, Mabel took more class photographs in front of the white clapboard entrance.

When Ann returned home from school, she found Sarah and Mabel inside the schoolhouse, arranging the desks into fewer rows. Their mother, still dressed in costume, had swapped her vintage lace-up, high-top shoes for her comfortable *clodhoppers*—the same grungy tennis shoes without the laces from years ago.

Sarah caught a glimpse of Ann and removed her calico bonnet, stuffing it inside the pocket of her matching pinafore. Skipping over to the teacher's desk, she retrieved the Polaroid pictures her mother had taken.

"So, how'd it go?"

"Come see for yourself," Sarah replied, motioning Ann forward. She propped up the photos in sequence along the chalkboard's narrow ledge. Ann spotted her sister's friend Melissa and a few other sixth-graders who rode their same school bus. Still, she didn't recognize most of the faces.

Motioning for Ann to follow, Sarah showed her their mother's thank you card and flowers, which Mabel had set on the sunny front stoop. "It was a blast, Annie! Maybe Mom will decide to open it up to high schoolers next year so you can do it, too."

"Yeah, maybe."

Kinda cool for little kids, but there's no way kids my age would dress up in silly outfits and play roles.

■ ■ ■

Spring break had already passed, but Mabel and Fred insisted on taking the girls on a four-day weekend to Clifton Valley, a quaint mountain town in the southwestern part of the state. Ann had learned long ago that questioning why something took place often led to her father's familiar warning: "Shush, we don't want to upset your mother!" So without playing investigator, she made arrangements to take her Chapter 12 biology test a day early and turn in her art portfolio on Tuesday rather than Friday.

Miss Mannis told Mabel that Sarah needn't worry about taking home assignments because she'd already skipped ahead of her classmates.

By Thursday evening, Fred had finished packing the car, and Mabel had crossed off the items on her to-do list.

Now in their bedrooms, the girls threw together tomorrow's outfits and gathered any odds and ends that might make the trip more bearable. They knew their father would rise before the roosters with his own *cock-a-doodle-doo*.

Sure enough, when morning arrived, Fred bellowed up the stairway. "Come on, girls, up and at 'em! We have a four-hour drive ahead of us, and if we're gonna make good time, we've gotta leave soon!"

Sarah groaned, rolling onto her stomach and placing her pillow over her head. She'd stayed up later than usual the last three nights, reading *Little Women*.

Ann reached over and turned on her bedside lamp, squinting to find her new John Lennon look-alike glasses so she could read the face on the alarm clock.

"Geez, Dad, it's five o'clock. What the heck?"

She swung her legs over the side of the bed and planted her bare feet on the rug. After a deep stretch and yawn, she put on her chenille robe and the pair of knee-high socks she'd set out the night before.

Ann paraded by Sarah's open doorway. "Hey, I smell bacon and pancakes. Last one downstairs is a loser!"

"How about the last one downstairs gets to sleep another fifteen minutes?" Sarah replied.

"Okay, loser!"

Fred's second stack of dollar-sized pancakes sat before him. "Good morning, young lady; pull up a chair and join me."

"Uh … good morning to you, too," Ann replied, snatching two pieces of bacon off the serving platter and taking a bite.

"Looks like you have an appetite as big as your father's this morning. How many pancakes would you like?" Mabel asked.

Ann hesitated, wondering why her mother seemed so unusually chipper. "How about two to start with?"

Mabel dipped the ladle into the batter. "Two fluffy blueberry pancakes coming right up."

Fred heard the sudden shuffle of Sarah's slippers on the kitchen linoleum and turned toward the doorway. "Well, look at who else has decided to join us on this fine morning!"

"Daddy, what's so fine about it? It's way too early!" Sarah rubbed the sleep from her eyes. "Why are we going to that town? What's it called, again? I forgot."

"Okay, you three, we need to save something to talk about for the car ride," Mabel said in her no-nonsense tone. She adjusted the waistband of her checkered apron. "Sarah, how many blueberry pancakes for you this morning?"

Sarah plopped down in her usual spot at the table, mouth downturned. "However many Annie's having. And do I have to go today? Maybe I could spend the weekend at Melissa's."

Ann found it hard to believe that their father didn't shush Sarah. He offered no stern look, no head shake, or no index finger held to his lips. Instead, he seemed preoccupied. *What's up with these two? They're both acting weird! Mother's hardly ever this nice, not to me anyway!*

■ ■ ■

Conversation carried on in waves. The lack of signs along the mountainous roadways made it difficult for the girls to play the Alphabet Game, and the small amount of traffic put a stop to playing Slug Bug. Instead, Sarah read *Little Women* while Ann shook her transistor radio in hopes of hearing something besides static.

Mabel knew the girls would need time to digest the forthcoming news. Nevertheless, she'd made it clear to Fred that he needn't put up with any 'ifs, ands, or buts.' As they neared the halfway point, she prodded him with a firm touch on his forearm.

"Ann Marie, Sarah, we have an announcement. Your mother and I have made a decision. We're ready for a change."

"You're not getting a divorce like my friend Larry's mom and dad, are you?" Sarah asked, leaning forward, eyes filled with fear.

Fred suppressed a laugh.

"No, nothing like that. It's good news. We're moving, the whole family, animals and all! Maybe even to Clifton Valley, the small town we'll be visiting today."

Silence followed. The girls didn't know how to respond to the news.

Ann's first thoughts zeroed in on friends left behind and adventures that would never happen. Both girls would've moved up to new Aurora public schools in the fall.

Ann stared out the window, lost in thought, grinding the toes of her sneakers into the floor mat.

This sucks! Screw 'em both! How can they do this to me?

What about Uncle Bob and Aunt Nell ... and Sammy? And what about Phillip?

He'll never have a chance to talk to me now.

Sarah sat glued to the window, *Little Women* closed and upside down on her lap.

■ ■ ■

Fred rounded the last long curve down Deer Hollow Pass. "We're in the home stretch, girls." Before them loomed Mt. Polk.

"My, look at that handsome slab of rock, would you? These are called the Presidential Peaks, girls, named after popular American presidents. And to the north of Mt. Polk, over there," he continued, pointing, "is Mt. Wilson. If we end up moving to this area, we'll have plenty of chances to do some exploring."

Time seemed to speed up.

Fred pulled into the parking lot at Mountain Meadows Real Estate on the south edge of Clifton Valley. Scott Goldman, the office broker—a tall scarecrow of a man in his mid-forties—had waited for their scheduled arrival. As they entered his office, he stood and extended his hand.

"Mr. and Mrs. Castle, welcome to Clifton Valley—Clifton for short. And these must be your daughters."

Fred introduced the girls. After which, Mr. Goldman wasted no time gathering keys and a multiple listings book before slipping on his windbreaker and ushering the Castles into his silver four-door sedan—Fred in the front passenger seat and Mabel and the girls in the back, Sarah sandwiched in between.

He turned the ignition.

"The first house we'll take a look at is a log rambler on thirteen acres, several miles from here across the street from Sunset Hill, our town cemetery."

Ann looked at Sarah with wide eyes of horror.

In a near whisper, she said, "No way. He's got to be kidding ... a cemetery? That's too all-fired creepy."

Moments later, Mr. Goldman wheeled the sedan up to the entrance gate of this first listing. Sarah shut her eyes, refusing to look over her shoulder at the cemetery grounds; however, its morbid enticement captured Ann's full attention.

The scape of uneven headstones corralled behind the ornate black wrought-iron fence drew her inside. Giant goosebumps popped up underneath the sleeves of her coat, and her body shivered.

As their realtor unlocked the front door, he prepared the Castles for the house tour. "Remember, folks, this house is rustic but has lots of character ... truly an original." He patted a bulky exterior log. "It was certainly built solid ... I believe, in 1939. And it's an absolute steal at this listing price."

He stepped back and held the door open.

The house's small footprint allowed for a quick walkthrough: one bedroom large enough for a double bed and moderate-sized dresser; a single bathroom, small by present standards, still sporting its original pink tile and white porcelain fixtures; a narrow living room with a handsome stone fireplace; a cramped u-shaped kitchen; and a separate, adequate-sized dining area.

Each room appeared clean and tidy yet needed a facelift.

On her way back outside, Mabel ran a hand along the varnished interior log walls. "These are beauties," she quietly said to no one in particular.

Mr. Goldman waited until the house had emptied and locked the front door.

He caught up to Fred and Mabel. "Now, as you can see, the grounds are impressive, quite spacious, which leaves room for expanding the house in all four directions. And I imagine you've noticed the meticulous upkeep."

Fred shielded his face from the noonday sun as he scanned the front yard, beginning with the blue spruce defining its southeastern edge. "Yes, Scott, their hard work shows."

Ann and Sarah lagged behind the adults, resigning themselves to the inevitable move. The squiggly creek cutting through the wooded pasture below the barnyard and the dozens of wagon-wheel gates and benches dotting the property had snagged Ann's interest.

Sarah leaned in close to her sister. "You know, Annie, this place *is* pretty cool. Maybe it wouldn't be so bad living here."

"Yeah, I suppose we'd get used to it. But do you have the guts to meet our *underground* neighbors at the cemetery?"

Sarah managed a brusque head shake.

To the west, behind the main house, stood a tiny A-frame cabin with the same bright-blue metal roof as the rest of the property's structures.

Mr. Goldman stopped and gestured widely with his hands.

"I've neglected to mention that this entire property was a sheep ranch throughout the '40s and '50s." He pointed to the cabin. "This building, which the owners built as a guesthouse in the early '60s, stands on the original site of a lambing shed."

Hmm, that's sorta cool.

The realtor stepped up to the front door of the A-frame. "Now the cabin's small but well laid out. The ground floor consists of a sitting room, a small kitchenette, and a full bathroom, while the attic serves as the sleep space with room for five."

He removed the master set of keys from his key ring and shook them enticingly at Ann and Sarah.

"Girls, you'll get a kick out of the wooden ladder attached to the wall, leading to the attic. As you'll see, there isn't enough room for stairs."

Mr. Goldman turned the key and pushed the solid-pine door wide open. To their parents' surprise, Ann and Sarah staked their claim on the cabin even though the south-facing attic window overlooked a corner of the cemetery grounds.

"Now, this is only a suggestion, Fred and Mabel," Mr. Goldman said as the group retraced its steps toward the house, "but it occurred to me that the cabin would make a cozy rental property for a single person."

Glancing sideways, he winked at Ann and Sarah.

"Sorry, girls, if I put the *kibosh* on your plans of moving into the cabin."

Ann's cheeks flushed.

"He gives me the creeps," she whispered to her sister as soon as he turned around.

Sarah nodded, eyes wide.

"The garage and barn are all that's left. Thank goodness!" Mr. Goldman stopped next in front of the detached two-car garage. "How about it, Fred ... do you have a garage back home?"

"No, sure don't, Scott, not even a carport." He peeked in through the side window. "I have to admit I wouldn't mind retiring the old ice scraper."

"Well, the honey in this garage has to be the large, separate room in the back. Allow me to show you," Mr. Goldman said, unlocking the room's exterior door.

Fred and Mabel agreed that the spacious area would serve nicely as a workshop for Fred's woodworking projects and her stained-glass hobby. And they both noted the extra storage space above the rafters throughout the entire garage.

A faded-red, two-story barn, the subject of many tourists' photos, stood adjacent to the garage. Ann watched Mabel eyeball its southeast exterior wall, an ideal location for an ample-sized chicken pen bathed in morning sunlight.

Why do Dad and Mother seem so excited to move? They spent so many years on the schoolhouse renovation. They're not going to move it, too, are they?

The entire move made little sense.

"Hey, Ann Marie, plenty of room for the horses, don't you think?" Fred asked from behind.

Ann turned and nodded. "Uh-huh. Did you see the tack room inside?"

"Not yet."

"It's cool ... kinda like Uncle Bob's. Follow me, and I'll show it to you."

Finally through, Mr. Goldman exited the barn behind the others, securing its wide-plank door with a heavy-duty padlock. "Well, folks, that's it for this property. Any other questions or something you'd like to see a second time?"

"Actually, Mabel and I would like to grab lunch with the girls and go over the notes I've taken. It might be that we'll discontinue our search and make an offer today on this place. You've mentioned there're several other interested parties."

"Yes, that's right, Fred." Mr. Goldman glanced at his watch. "It's eleven-forty. How about we meet back at my office around ... say ... one o'clock?"

■ ■ ■

Late Monday afternoon, with contract papers signed, the Castles left the mountain passes behind and headed back toward the plains. Mabel had registered Ann to begin her sophomore year at Clifton Valley High School in the fall and Sarah the town's middle school.

Fred had confirmed his pending change in work schedule with Rhineholdt—report to work at the Denver plant on Monday mornings and return to Clifton after each Thursday's workday. Mabel planned to contact an assertive real estate broker the next morning to list the farm and had decided that the schoolhouse would remain open to the Aurora Public School system through May.

Sarah skimmed over a *Seventeen Magazine* the girls had bought at All Foods Market in Clifton while Ann closed her eyes and half-heartedly listened to Fred and Mabel mull over their latest to-do list. Her mother's occasional complaints passed through Ann's ears with little notice as she thought about making her own to-do list.

Much later, Ann woke up to the sound of her father's car door slamming shut.

Sarah popped her knuckles in her sister's ear. "We're home, Annie. Look who's the loser now!"

"Quit it." She batted at Sarah's arm but missed. "Man, I didn't mean to fall asleep. What did I miss?"

"Believe me, not a thing."

"All right, girls, I want you to help carry everything inside," Mabel said. "And not just one trip. Do you hear me?"

"Okay," they replied in unison.

Fred opened the backend and handed Sarah her first load before slinging his canvas duffle bag over his shoulder and grabbing Mabel's Samsonite suitcase. "All right, Sarah, let's drop this first bunch off inside the front door."

Mabel stepped around to the back of the car.

"Here, Ann Marie, this box isn't too heavy."

Removing the box from her mother's firm hold, she asked, "Do Uncle Bob and Aunt Nell know we're moving?"

"Heavens, no! When would I have had time to talk to them?"

Ann looked at the ground and said under her breath, "Geez, I wish I could go live with them."

"What'd you say, Ann Marie?"

"Nothing."

Mabel's eyes narrowed to crescent moons as she grabbed hold of Ann's chin. "*What* did you say?"

"I didn't say anything, Mom. Nothing important."

"I'm sick and tired of you treating me like dirt under your feet, Ann Marie!" Mabel drew her hand back and slapped the box from Ann's grip. "Next time, it'll be your face … got it?" She moved closer. "I'm ready to have you go live with your uncle and aunt! Is that what you want?"

Clenching both fists, she resumed, "Huh, is it? And for Pete's sake, quit your slouching and stand up straight! You're such a sight! Turtle!"

Ann bent over and turned the box upright on the ground, dusting off the few spilled items. She willed herself not to cry.

"No, Mother, it's not what I want."

Of course, it is. In a heartbeat. You'll never know how much I hate it here. And how much I hate you.

■ ■ ■

After double-checking that she had the next day's school outfit decided, her art portfolio ready to turn in, and her hot lunch ticket tucked inside her wallet, Ann removed a sheet of college-ruled notebook paper from a binder on the bottom shelf of her bookcase. In her best cursive hand, she wrote 'Priority List' across the top of the page before numbering from one to twenty-five vertically down the left-hand margin.

Ann stopped writing and looked sideways at her bedroom door. "Sarah, is that you? Did you knock?"

"Yeah, it's me," she answered softly. "Can I come in?"

"Sure."

Sarah stepped inside and closed the door.

"I heard Mom yelling at you earlier."

"Yeah, well, you and everyone else for miles—"

"You know, Annie, you're not the only one she yells at and smacks."

"Huh? What're you talking about?"

"I'm telling you she loses her temper with me, too. And most of the time, I don't know why. Things seem okay ... then she blows up. She's whacked me a few times ... mostly with wooden spoons or the flyswatter."

"You're kidding! Right?"

"I wish."

Ann's features twisted in disbelief. She shook her head. "But you're her precious *little princess*. And don't you dare deny it, Sarah."

Sarah shrugged, face expressionless. "Not anymore; not since I became friends with Melissa."

All of a sudden, in an about-face, Ann giggled. "Maybe, instead of flyswatters or switches, she'll use the horrible teacher's paddle hanging up at the schoolhouse!"

With fists on her hips, Sarah replied in a deep, gruff voice, "You mean 'the board of education,'" making her sister snort. "I don't know about you, but I'd rather wear the dunce hat and sit in the corner."

"Yeah!" Ann said, nodding. "And I can also see her grabbing us by the earlobes like mean people on TV do and shoving us into the schoolhouse as punishment."

"And if we're good, Annie, maybe she'll give us bread and water."

"There's an old saying," Ann said, peering at the ceiling. "Something about 'out of sight ... out of mind.' It's a good thing our teachers and friends might miss us at school!"

The girls laughed and shared an awkward hug, gangly arms clenched tight.

Although it was tough for Sarah to admit to her mother's harsh treatment, the news came as a blessed relief for Ann. Now, maybe she could stop hating her sister.

Chapter Ten

November 1972

Finding a niche within the rigid small-town social structure of the Clifton public schools proved much harder for Ann than for Sarah. With Sarah's personality set to *full power*, she singlehandedly blasted through the junior high cliques of her choice, while Ann latched onto another newcomer in hopes of reducing her anxiety over trying to fit in. She and Yvonne, who'd moved to the valley around the same time—a pair of sour notes in an otherwise synchronized flow of melodies—took refuge in their easy friendship against the harsh whispers and stares first received from several of the other girls. In due time, however, a steady rhythm developed, and the tension between the two newcomers and their fellow students played itself out.

■ ■ ■

The varsity football team's 8-2 record had propelled them into the regional championship game. In celebration, dozens of students armed with blue paint and magic markers transformed reams of butcher paper into banners lining the hallways and auditorium.

Along Center Street, royal blue and silver streamers framed doorways and window fronts while balloon bunches, the same regal school colors, bobbed above available poles and lampposts. Throughout town flowed a river of blue and silver—from T-shirts and pants to dresses and shirts, from suits and ties to shorts and skorts, and from caps and scarves to the occasional full-blown painted male torso.

The afternoon's high school pep rally exuded tremendous energy and school spirit. Students didn't want the festivities to end—the band continued to play, the Pep Club carried on with its latest chant, and the varsity cheerleaders kept at their new, original cheer.

However, the principal couldn't ignore the final bell, and after a loud "Go Cougars!" into the microphone and a hand signal to cut the rally short, he dismissed the bus riders first.

Several Pep Club members invited Ann and Yvonne, the newest club fledglings, to tag along to the Trail's End Café for a soda and fries, followed by cruising around town. Both girls used the payphone in the lobby outside the gym to check in with their mothers. Mabel ordered Ann home by dusk, which she translated to five o'clock.

She also warned that no *wiggle room* would be tolerated.

Ann looked at her watch. *Okay, this is doable. Mmm, I can almost smell the fries!*

Other students had the same idea. Once seated, service in the crowded café continued at its quick and synchronized pace, not a single step wasted. Ann watched as the open kitchen worked its magic. The sight of the short-order cooks flipping burger patties, foot-long dogs, and Vidalia onion slices on the grill made her stomach growl. And the smell of the hot grease from the deep fryer brought a childlike grin to her face

Soon the waitress placed the girls' orders on the table. Ann quickly took a gulp from her frosted root beer mug, licking the foam off her lips. *Yeah, that hits the spot!*

Picking up a crispy, crooked fry from the heap on her plate, she folded it in half and gave it several quick blows. Its scent caused a sudden attack of sentimentality, transporting her back to Mike's Tavern, Uncle Bob at her side.

"Here, dip it in my ketchup," Yvonne said, pushing her plate toward her friend.

Ann dragged the fry through the reservoir of Heinz 57 that Yvonne had dumped along the rim and popped it into her mouth. "Thanks."

This one's for you and me, Uncle Bob!

Neither Ann nor Yvonne said much.

Instead, both newcomers shifted around in their seats, fingering their tableware while the other three girls traded inside jokes and bits of gossip regarding who dated whom and who had to serve detention. Ann noticed that Yvonne had folded her napkin to the size of a crumpled postage stamp. She caught Yvonne's gaze and smiled, holding up her napkin, a misshapen cigar.

With plates picked clean and the bill paid, the fivesome left the restaurant.

Feeling duty-bound to the time, Ann checked her watch once again. Still early, she looked forward to looping around town and dragging up and down East Center with the rest of the girls. She made a mental note to remind Betz to head toward her house by a quarter to five.

As fifteen-year-olds, Ann and Yvonne's usual modes of transportation consisted of car rides with a parent at the wheel, the school bus, bicycles, or doubles on Lucky. The opportunity for the duo to hang out with a girl who had a driver's license and access to a car had never before occurred. "Wow, I can't believe Betz's brother would let her use his Mustang," Yvonne said to Ann in a hushed voice, brushing the bronze metallic hood with her fingertips. "If I had an older brother, Annie, I betcha he wouldn't let me anywhere near his car!"

Before Betz could pull open the heavy passenger door, Phyllis laid claim to the front seat. Ann, Yvonne, and Janie scooted into the back.

"Hey, guys, let me take your picture." Phyllis pulled her Kodak Instamatic from her coat pocket and turned in her seat, facing the back. "Okay, Annie and Janie, move closer to Yvonne," she said, watching through the viewfinder. "Perfect!"

She snapped the photo and advanced the film before flopping back around in the bucket seat. A swift turn of the key produced a nearly inaudible *purr*. "Hey, Phyllis, we need music in here," Betz said, tapping the steering wheel with both palms. "Grab an eight-track out of the glove box, will you?"

"Sure." The small door dropped open. "Which one? There're several in here."

"Ooh, *Led Zeppelin IV*—the one with 'Stairway to Heaven.'"

Phyllis popped the tape into the player.

Betz swayed to the seductive melody as she sang along. "Okay, where to, you guys?"

"Follow Dave and Eric!" Janie said, pointing to the red Jeep on the far side of the parking lot. "See, they're pulling out onto Mountain View. Ooh, Dave's so cool! I heard he and Mary broke up last night. I'm pretty sure she wasn't wearing his class ring this morning in Algebra."

"Sounds like maybe you have a thing for him, Janie!" said Phyllis.

Janie batted her eyes. "Well, maybe I do!"

Ann and Yvonne looked at each other and laughed.

"Okay, hang on!" Betz said as she peeled out of the parking lot.

Janie scooted down in the seat. "Don't be so obvious!"

"And don't you be such a wuss, Janie," Betz replied with a playful smile. She glanced into the rearview mirror and relaxed her foot off the gas pedal.

East Center Street teemed with high schoolers in automobiles. Honks and jubilant shouts accompanied the impromptu parade. Betz followed the cluster of cars up, down, and around the main stretch until Phyllis spotted Dave and Eric break away from the pack and head toward the park.

Janie leaned forward. "I asked you not to be so damned obvious, Betz!"

"Hell, Janie, the last time I checked, it was still a public park."

Phyllis leaned over and patted Betz's arm. "Good one!"

"Well, aren't you two girls funny? You're both so freakin' funny the rest of us forgot to laugh," Janie said, a bite to her tone.

Ann responded with a nervous giggle, uncertain if the girls' exchange had turned bitter. Betz parked in the first available space, and she and Phyllis jumped out, pulling their seats forward.

"I hate to ask, Betz," Ann said as she leaned toward the open door, top lip clenched between her teeth, "but I'm going to need a ride home in a few minutes."

"Oh, that's right, I forgot."

"Do you mind if we go over and see what Ellie's up to first?" asked Betz, pointing ahead. "She's driving the Camaro parked over there by the picnic table. Have you met her yet?"

Before Ann could answer, Betz turned and ran toward Ellie, her hand waving through the air. Phyllis and Janie led the way.

"Great!" Ann said to Yvonne. "What in the world do I do now?"

"Well, you either wait or walk home. I vote you wait a few minutes."

"Okay … I hope my mother isn't counting down the minutes. Ugh! My ass is gonna be grass!"

The girls hopped out the open driver's door. They walked past Dave and Eric, who leaned against Dave's Jeep, talking animatedly to three older boys the girls didn't know. Ann kept glancing at the Camaro, but no one moved.

Dusk rapidly approached.

Why can't I catch a break? And why does Dad have to be in Boston? Although what kinda help would he be anyway? He never stands up to her or sticks up for me.

Ann looked at her watch before glancing at Yvonne.

"If I run, Yvonne, I might make it home on time!"

Yvonne patted Ann's arm. "Good luck! I'll tell Betz you couldn't wait any longer!"

As Ann turned from West Center onto Steele Street in a half-walk, half-run, her lungs nearly burst before her trembling legs carried her up the hill. Exhaustion gave way to panic as she spotted her mother standing by the entry gate to the driveway. Reluctantly, she carried on.

"You're late, young lady! Get over here!"

Clutching Ann's forearm, she produced a thick cottonwood branch from behind her back. Eyes wide and nostrils flaring, she whacked the backs of her daughter's thighs.

Ann refused to rip loose from her mother's fierce grip or block the lashes with her hands. Rather than giving Mother the satisfaction, she gritted her teeth and choked back all response.

In her frenzied state, Mabel didn't notice the Mustang as it slowed and swerved past them. Ann caught Phyllis's surprised look out the passenger window and thought she mouthed the word "sorry." But in the dark, she couldn't be certain.

After grounding Ann for the next two weeks, Mabel, still fuming, lobbed the branch to the side of the gate and stormed into the house.

With much clanging of utensils and banging of cupboard doors, she proceeded to dish up a bowl of beef chili and a buttered roll for herself.

Ann slipped past the kitchen and retreated to Sarah's and her bedroom, angry, exhausted, and ready for sleep. Body trembling, she stripped off her dark-blue corduroy pants, gingerly fingering the rising welts on the back of both thighs. With a heavy sigh, she peeled off her sweat-soaked turtleneck and changed into her baggy flannel PJs.

As Ann turned toward the double bed, which she reluctantly shared with her sister, she caught her reflection in the full-length mirror attached to the closet door.

She spun around, aligned herself in front of it, and scrutinized her boyish frame from top to bottom.

"Sarah's boobs are ten times bigger. Mine look like friggin' mosquito bites! And look, I have no waist."

Leaning closer to the mirror, she studied her rounded shoulders, first one and then the other. Next, with a mixture of curiosity and disbelief, she watched her reflection as it took a closed fist and delivered a half-dozen quick, hard raps to her head. *I hate you! You're so freakin' stupid and ugly! Look at you, Turtle! No wonder your bitch-mother can't stand you!*

She tried to force herself to cry, but the tears wouldn't come.

Instead, she stumbled over to the bottom drawer of the maple dresser, plucking out a ragtag-stuffed basset hound, sad-faced and long-neglected, and her threadbare satin baby blanket not long ago given up. She pulled them close and crawled into bed, positioning herself in the middle, thankful not to battle Sarah's flailing limbs tonight as she had permission to spend the night at a girlfriend's house.

Ann shut out all thoughts of Mabel. Rather, she contemplated her lost friendship with Sammy and how what she shared with Yvonne paled in comparison.

She also recalled her favorite memories of Uncle Bob and Aunt

Nell, decided to stop pining for Phillip, and made a promise to spend more time with Lucky.

Soon, dreamless sleep nabbed her.

■ ■ ■

The previous day's grounding kept Ann home from the regional championship game. Grudgingly, she followed Mabel's strict orders to keep the radio turned off and learned of the finger-gnawing, hair-pulling 28 to 27 loss from Sarah.

"Here, Annie, do you want my pennant?" Sarah asked, unfurling the small triangle of blue-and-white felt with the silver lettering from around the narrow dowel. She held it out to Ann like a form of penance for once again playing the *good-daughter* role.

Seated on their bed, a hangdog expression plastered on her face, Ann bobbed her head and took it from her sister's gloved hand. "Did Yvonne ask about me?"

"Yeah, she also said not to count on riding around with Betz anymore."

"Well, that's not a big surprise," Ann replied, flopping onto her side, away from Sarah.

■ ■ ■

After returning from Christmas vacation, Ann's homeroom teacher, Mrs. Tucker—a tall, ardent blonde who could persuade even the most unlikely student to diagram a complex sentence—pulled her aside.

She explained that she was on a recruiting mission for new reporters for *The Cougars' Chronicle*, the school newspaper. She saw in Ann a budding investigative journalist waiting to break into *the biz*.

Ann responded with an emphatic, "Why not?"

Her first assignment was an interview with Greg Richards, high school senior and Ski Club president, at the club's first bi-monthly meeting that afternoon.

Ann knew little about skiing, but with Mrs. Tucker's help, she wrote a handful of general questions.

"Just remember, Ann, have fun with the interview. If you don't understand part of an answer, rephrase the question. And I'll help you write the first couple of articles until you feel comfortable doing it alone."

"Okay. Thanks!"

"Now, go get 'em!" Mrs. Tucker clapped her hands overhead, cheering Ann on.

Ann spotted Greg setting up chairs in a semi-circle in the northwest corner of the lunchroom. She walked over to him while coaching herself to breathe, stay calm, and remember that he seemed a nice enough guy.

"Hi, Greg," Ann said with a croak, clearing her throat. "I don't know if you remember me. I'm Ann Castle ... I was in your biology class last quarter." She pulled her notebook up to her chin, cheeks painted coral.

"Yeah, of course, I do. Mrs. Tucker told me you'd be coming by to ask me some questions for *The Cougars' Chronicle*."

"Yeah? You're my first interview." She hesitated, teetering on the balls of her feet. "Is it okay to ask you the questions now?"

"Sure, go ahead. But I'm gonna have to finish setting up while we talk. A few of the guys come early."

"All right." Ann pulled the cap off her pen and rested her spiral notebook against her forearm. *Hmm ... maybe I should enunciate my words like TV newscasters do. Nah, that's stupid!* "So, Greg, how long have you been a skier?"

Greg lined up a third row of chairs, talking above the clanking of their metal legs against the yellowed linoleum. "Oh, let's see ... I was five years old. My parents bought my first pair of skis for my birthday that year. So that would make it twelve years. Do you ski?"

"No, not anymore. I tried it once in junior high, but I fell and dislocated my knee. I'm such a klutz ... my little sister's pretty good, though."

Geez, I didn't need to say all that!
I bet my dork status hit the roof!

"You ought to take it up again."

"Maybe." Ann glanced at the scuff marks on her shoes to hide her flaming cheeks. "And ... um ... how long has the club been in existence?"

"I should know right off the bat, but I'll have to think for a minute." Greg looked toward the ceiling and counted on his fingers. "Me, Jack, Rachel, Tom, and ... Mary Mueller." He turned toward Ann. "Okay, if I remembered the past presidents correctly, the answer would be five years. Yeah, sounds right."

Ann recorded the answer.

"What's the club's purpose?"

"Well, mainly to provide discounted ski passes and low-cost transportation for kids like me, I guess." Greg shrugged. "And, of course, we get better the more weeks we go. Plus, skiing is a shitload .... oops, I mean a truckload of fun!"

Ann jumped as a stocky boy in a blue Cougars sweatshirt blasted his way into the lunchroom through the exterior utility door.

"Hey there, Prez!" he hollered from across the room.

Greg motioned in his direction, a broad grin radiating across his face.

Ann sensed Greg's impatience. "One more, okay?" she asked, her body curling into itself.

"Sure, shoot."

"Um ... how would a student go about joining Ski Club?"

"They can either talk to me or Mr. Feldman, our teacher sponsor, or come to a meeting. There's a new club calendar on the bulletin board outside the guidance office." Greg turned and walked over toward the boy in the team sweatshirt, now horsing around with the other students who'd trickled into the lunchroom.

"Thanks, Greg!" Ann said in a syrupy voice.

Great, he probably thinks I'm a brownnoser or, even worse, a big flirt!

"Yep, anytime," he replied, looking straight ahead.

Ann closed her notebook without recording Greg's last answer. She could feel a number of eyes focused on her as she turned and moved toward the main cafeteria entrance.

A sarcastic male voice, one that Ann didn't recognize, filled the cafeteria.

"Hey, man, why talk to the *hunchback*? She should join the circus!"

The boy's coarse chuckles punched her hard between her shoulder blades.

Her steps quickened, and she refused to turn around.

By the time Ann reached the hallway, her shoulder muscles burned as hot as if splayed over a barbeque grill. Her attempt to pull them back and minimize the unsightly hump proved fruitless.

Ann stopped at her locker and opened the door, fighting to hold back tears. Her thoughts slowed, trapped in the thick mud that had become her brain.

"Hey, Annie, what's up with you? You look like you've lost your best friend. But hey, that's me!" Yvonne said, rosy face beaming. "Put your notebook away and come walk with me. I've had the best day ever, and I want to tell you about it!"

Yvonne, oblivious to her friend's mournful sigh, watched as Ann tossed the notebook on the bottom of her locker and shut the door with a *bang.*

Ann swallowed hard and, in a singsong voice, answered, "Sure, Yvonne. What was so good about your day? Please tell me."

You don't want to hear about my glorious day; I guarantee it.

"Look, there's something taped to your locker." Yvonne took hold of the right-hand corner and pulled. "Ha! It's the picture of you, me, and Janie in the backseat of Betz's brother's Mustang! The one Phyllis took." She glanced at Ann, bemused. "Didn't you see it when you opened the door?"

Ann didn't answer. She took the photo from Yvonne and dropped it into the middle section of her purse. "I'll look at it later. Now, what were you going to tell me? Does it have to do with a certain boy named Dan?"

"Yes, how did you know? Do you have EPS?"

"You mean ESP?" *Oh, brother!* "Come on, Yvonne. Let's walk and talk."

The two merged into the slapdash flow of students and faculty. Ann forced herself to swallow the rude boy's words, and after exhaling the rest of her woes, she slipped on her *best-friend mask,* focusing on Yvonne's animated tale of her day's events.

Chapter Eleven

September 1975 – May 1976

During Ann's senior year of high school, she accepted the student editor position of *The Cougars' Chronicle*—a fancy title equating to nothing more than a glorified messenger. Her primary responsibility remained the delivery of the student reporters' articles on the first and third Wednesdays of the month to the *Clifton Valley News,* where employees set and printed them on their antiquated Linotype hot-metal press.

Other duties included picking up the printed copies the following afternoon for Friday's seventh-period distribution and collecting advertising copy from local businesses and club sponsors.

The title brought Ann no more assignments than the rest of the student reporters, no special passes to local town events, and no prestige, which suited her fine.

But according to Yvonne, the position *had* served to boost her confidence.

She regularly reminded Ann that guys 'who have it together' prefer girls 'who have it together.'

When Ann first discussed accepting the student-editor role with Fred and Mabel, the consensus stood clear: "You better wear good shoes because you'll have a lot of miles to cover!"

But they soon softened and offered her the use of Grandpa Castle's '48 Chevy pickup truck, which, although refurbished, had sat idle since Fred purchased the new Impala for his weekly roundtrip business commute to Denver. No stranger to the truck's sticky clutch, lack of power steering, and rough shift into reverse, Ann felt ecstatic. Her hours of practice spent driving it down the hardpan dirt roads around the rural Aurora farm, on Fred or Mabel's lap first and then solo, now proved useful.

Ann's borrowed set of wheels, which she'd dubbed Bubba the Beast, attracted a fair number of stares and comments from the male gender as she traveled around town collecting the advertising copy for Mrs. Tucker. Old Mr. Hagan from the hardware store—who often told the story of teaching his two boys to drive in a classic '48 Ford F-1 pickup painted a similar brick-red as Bubba—never ceased to advise Ann to give him a jingle once she decided to sell the 'old jalopy.' And Del Simpson of Del's Diner never failed to wave a thumbs-up when Ann steered Bubba up to the curb. But Tim Palmer, assistant manager of All Foods Market, his father's business of twenty-nine years, remained whom Ann most wanted to take notice of her and her *ride*. His quick head nod and slightly crooked smile turned her insides upside down, and she found it difficult to talk to him without sputtering like a clogged-up sprinkler.

By combing through the earlier Clifton Valley High School annuals at the school's library, Ann learned that Tim graduated in 1970 and decided he'd grown more handsome since then, especially with his thick blond mane cut short. She noted with enthusiasm that he had played defensive linebacker on the varsity football team during his last two years of high school and participated in all-state his senior year. She also counted membership in four clubs the year he graduated. Nevertheless, her greatest delight came from learning that he remained single—information gleaned from Yvonne's mother, a school library volunteer and part-time cashier at All Foods Market.

Ann calculated a six-year age difference between them if Tim graduated at eighteen years old. She knew Uncle Bob and Aunt Nell's age difference stood at five years and that Yvonne dated a college junior. Six years seemed like nothing.

■ ■ ■

As Ann wheeled Bubba into the last available parking space on the south side of All Foods Market, she spotted Tim and another employee rounding up stray carts in the alley.

She waved and took several deep breaths before climbing out of the truck, wishing she'd checked her face and hair in the visor mirror before leaving the school parking lot.

"Hey there, Ann; is it Wednesday already?" Tim asked, returning a wave.

"Yep, I'm afraid so." She moved her clipboard to her right hand and wiped her sweaty left palm on the back of her jeans, out of Tim's sight.

"Well, follow me into my office. I have the advertising copy all ready for you."

Ann searched for something casual to say as she trailed after Tim through the back door and up the stairs to his office.

She considered mentioning the weather, but who'd want to discuss snowfall statistics?

And she knew too little about professional football and other sports.

Furthermore, Ann figured it a blunder to admit that she could faint when he said her name or that she swooned over the thought of him kissing her passionately like a handsome hero in a classic black-and-white movie.

Ann's stomach did a double summersault.

Tim held the door open to his office at the top of the steps. "Come in. It'll only take me a second to grab it." He plucked the new ad copy from the top drawer of the gunmetal-colored file cabinet next to his desk and handed it to Ann.

"Hmm, the layout's different this time," she said as she glanced at his now-recognizable block letters, neatly penciled and perfectly spaced.

"Yeah, we're celebrating the market's thirtieth anniversary on Saturday, November 16, with an open house, and I've included an announcement. We'll also be putting a large ad in the *Clifton Valley News* with a similar announcement. Anyway, please have Mrs. Tucker call me if she has any questions, okay?"

Ann attached the advertising copy to her clipboard. "Yes, I sure will."

"I hope you and your parents will plan on coming. There'll be food and door prizes."

"Yes, that sounds great. I'll make it a point to tell them." Ann waved. "Thanks, Tim. I know my way out." As Tim's door clicked shut, she said to herself, "Ha! There's no way they'll be coming with me."

Ann held the clipboard against her chest and pulled her shoulders back as best she could. With a sense of urgency tugging her forward, she fixed her eyes on the black-and-white linoleum flooring and sailed down the steps to the front of the store, past the checkout stands, and out the main entrance. The two parking spaces on either side of Bubba had emptied. Ann stepped up onto the running board and climbed in. Hurriedly, she lowered the visor, removed her glasses, and pulled on her right cheek. "My mascara's smudged. Great, I look like a stupid raccoon!"

Glimpsing her newly feathered bangs and tight ponytail, she smiled. "At least my hair looks good!"

And maybe he didn't notice my hunched back so much with my jacket on.

■ ■ ■

The day's temperature, mild for mid-November, called for something lighter than Ann's heavy coat. She stood in front of the full-length mirror, deciding what she could wear over her burgundy jumper and matching short-sleeved blouse.

She first threw on a gray sweater, adjusting the sleeves and shoulder seams. "Looks good from the front, but the back accentuates my blessed hump!"

She stuck her tongue out at her reflection. "Ugh! I look like a friggin' carnival freak!"

Hastily, she tossed the sweater across the foot of the bed, slipped on the black jacket she'd made last year in Home Economics class, and stood sideways.

Hmm ... better. The sleeves are a bit short, though.

She scrunched them up to her elbows, deciding that would have to do.

While straightening the lapels, she checked her makeup in the mirror one last time. Finally, she removed her black vinyl purse from the long hook on the back of the closet door, placing it over her left shoulder cross-wise like they did in the magazines. *Ha! If the outfit were green, I'd look like a Girl Scout! Oh, well, too late.*

By the time Ann arrived at All Foods Market for the tail end of the Open House, a half-dozen people milled around the area partitioned off for the special event.

Tim, dressed in a dark suit and wide burgundy tie, stood at the refreshment table, serving from the third and final frosted sheet cake. Next to the cake, in a massive crystal punch bowl, a frozen pineapple ring melted in a shallow pool of Hawaiian Punch.

Ann adjusted the back of her jacket before clasping her hands in front of her.

She walked past the stragglers toward the serving table.

Please, the rest of you, go home! Come on; give me a chance, would you?

Tim stood over the cake, ready to plate up another slice.

She spoke in a soft voice so as not to startle him. "Congratulations, Tim. By the looks of what's left of the refreshments, you had a good turnout."

Tim's head sprung up like a page in a pop-up book. "Well, hi, Ann." He placed the stainless-steel cake knife on an empty paper plate and brushed his hands against one another. "Yeah, it's been so busy I haven't had a chance to sit down all afternoon. Hey, would you join me for a piece of cake?"

"Sure, Tim. Why not?"

"Good. I'll plate the cake if you want to grab a couple of forks and napkins." He chose two chairs close to the serving table.

Ann emptied her mouth before speaking. "So, how many people stopped by?"

"Well, Dad and I figure around 250," Tim replied, wiping his bottom lip with his glossy silver napkin.

"Wow! Is that the number you were hoping for?"

"Yeah, we're pleased. I imagine—"

"Excuse me for interrupting, Tim, but the reporter from the *Clifton Valley News* finally made it for the interview and photos. Can you break away for a few minutes?" asked Al, Tim's father, his hands planted on the back of his son's chair.

Tim shrugged. "Sure, Dad, I'll be right there."

He stood and touched Ann's forearm with a short sigh of apology.

"Sorry! Duty calls. I look forward to seeing you on Wednesday, though."

Ann's heart beat so hard that she feared it might be visible through her jacket. "That sounds good. See you then."

She finished her last bite of cake while the reporter positioned the two men, along with several long-time employees, behind the serving table for photographs. Suddenly, Ann decided to take a picture for the school newspaper.

She fished around in her purse and snagged her camera.

Careful not to get in the way, she stepped off to the side and snapped two photos—one for *The Cougars' Chronicle* and one for herself. She marveled at how Tim simply looked like a younger version of his father. Neither the term clean-cut nor pretty boy fit their looks. *Ruggedly handsome* rang true, she decided.

■ ■ ■

By the time February rolled around, Clifton's deep freeze had lasted for two weeks. Daytime temperatures hovered around zero, and nighttime temperatures continued to dip into the minus-twenty-degree range.

Fred had temporarily put his commuting on hold, doing what he could by phone from home. In addition, he kept busy helping Mabel tend to the animals or ferrying the family around town in the Impala when Bubba or the station wagon refused to start.

The frigid weather kept Ann and Sarah at home in the evenings, away from extracurricular activities. To compensate, Sarah finagled her father into regular afterschool showdowns of cribbage or checkers while Ann chose to burrow under the bedcovers with her many spiral notebooks and colored pencils. She now considered herself too old to keep a diary.

Instead, she often made entries in her *Feelings Journal*. Occasionally, she wrote a short story or added the final verses to an unfinished poem. But most often, she let her thoughts dance wild and free across the page:

L oad your heart with loving kindness.
O ffer it to those who cross your path. (Tim!)
V alue yourself and all of life around you. (Tim!)
E specially those who show you wrath. (Mother!)

Oh, Tim, your startling blue eyes make my heart pound! You're my 'mister right'!
Mr. and Mrs. Tim Palmer
*Ann Palmer * Annie Palmer * Mrs. Ann Marie Palmer*

In addition to the usual freezing temperatures, each February marked the busy time in the high school's guidance office when all seniors began a required series of individual meetings with Mr. Pullman, the guidance counselor.

During these meetings, he encouraged students to explore colleges, trade schools, or job options tailored to their particular interests and aptitudes.

Ann found her name written in the day's first appointment slot. She greeted Mrs. Kountze, Mr. Pullman's secretary, a fierce-looking, middle-aged woman with a robust snowman of a figure. Tongue-tied, she mispronounced her last name, saying "Cattle" instead of Castle.

Mrs. Kountze drew a wavy line through Ann's name, printed in capitals. She looked up over small half-glasses. "Please take a—"

"Good morning, Ann," Mr. Pullman interrupted. "Come into my office and have a seat." He extended his sturdy right hand and pointed to the dingy vinyl chair across from his desk.

"Thank you," Ann replied, cheeks reddening. She sat down, unsure of what to expect. Neither Yvonne nor the few other classmates who'd already completed their first meetings had had much to say when she'd asked them about their experiences.

Mr. Pullman adjusted his black horn-rimmed glasses and removed Ann's file from the top of the manila mountain on his desk.

"Very good," he said, glancing at the first page. "It looks like you're on target with your credits and will be eligible to graduate on time. And at this point, you're ranked in the top third of your graduating class. Good for you." He put the folder down. "Tell me, Ann, have you and your parents given any consideration to what you'd like to do after graduation?"

Ann's face dropped like a fifty-pound weight.

"Um ... well ... no, Mr. Pullman, they talk to my sister once in a while about going to nursing school, but they've never said anything about me going to college. We hardly ever discuss my grades or anything else to do with my high school classes." She grasped a strand of hair and wrapped it around her finger, staring at the shiny pennies wedged inside the slits of her loafers.

I'm probably the only one in the whole school who doesn't have a clue. "I'm sorry! I have to admit I haven't given it too much thought."

Mr. Pullman picked up Ann's folder once again and thumbed through the rest of the pages. "Let's see what this is," he said, removing a half-sheet of paper clipped to the back of the file. Ann shifted in her seat and watched his ribbon-thin lips move as he silently read through the memo. "Well, Ann, this is from Mrs. Tucker. She seems to think you're a talented writer and would make a top-notch journalism student. She's even provided information on several journalism scholarships. What do you think?"

Ann donned a sheepish grin and shrugged. "Well, Mr. Pullman,

I do like to write articles for *The Cougars' Chronicle*. Working at a professional newspaper would be exciting. I can ask my mother and dad about it tonight."

"Good, Ann! Let's schedule another appointment for a week from today at the same time. Meanwhile, I'll gather more information on journalism scholarships."

Mr. Pullman pulled an appointment card from the top drawer of his desk, filled in the blanks, and handed it to her. "Okay, I'll see you next week. Please talk with your parents."

"I will. Thanks, Mr. Pullman." Ann dropped the appointment card into the zipper compartment of her purse as he opened the door.

She didn't understand why the other students hadn't had much to say after meeting with Mr. Pullman. Clearly an insightful man, she felt that he had honestly tried to help her.

And now, maybe she could get a career started! Who'd have thought?

The rest of the school day progressed at a slow pace, Ann's thoughts often pulling away from schoolwork, hopping back and forth between how to become Tim's girlfriend and how to bring up the matter of college with her parents.

By the final bell, however, after recalling those haunting, hurtful words her mother had uttered to the Aurora librarian years ago, Ann had decided to bury the subject of college. *Yeah, Mother, I may not be college material.*

Your words were 'successful material,' weren't they? You were going around, all high and mighty, predicting that I wouldn't make it in a real profession.

Not like your dear little Sarah, the future nurse!

Right, Mother? Huh? Tell me! Ewwww, I hate you!

And, Dad, you let her get away with hen-pecking you all the time ... *going along with what she says. You two watch; Tim's going to fall in love with me, hunched back and all, and ask me to marry him.*

Then I can escape from home! You'll see.

Who needs stupid college anyway?

When the school bell stopped ringing, Ann found herself grinding her teeth and making a fist. She glanced around, hoping no one in her class had noticed. Crouching, she collected her coat from the back of the chair and slid out the door.

■ ■ ■

As the weather forecasters had predicted with their customary clichés, March "came in like a ferocious lion" and "exited like a docile lamb." April showers followed, bringing about an explosion of color in time for Clifton Valley High's graduation ceremony.

By the ceremony's end, much of the audience had already vacated the auditorium, eager to avoid the inevitable traffic bottleneck along Center Street. Mabel asked Bob and Nell to join Ann in front of the stage for a picture before she and Fred found Sarah and left for home. It took three tries before the bulb flashed.

Alone at last with her uncle and aunt, Ann took hold of their hands and squeezed. "Thanks again for coming! I know it's a long drive."

"Honey, we wouldn't have missed your graduation for the world." Nell kissed Ann on the cheek. "You know, Annie, your uncle and I still laugh when we look back on all those crazy talent shows the three of us put on the summer you stayed with us. That was a grand time."

Bob, his thin hair mostly white, gave Ann a big bear hug that lingered for both to savor. "Annie, I wish we didn't have to take off for the ranch, but I'm glad we had a nice visit this morning. You'll let Aunt Nell and me know if you get the newspaper job selling ads, won't you? We know you'll be good at anything you put your mind to."

"Yes, I promise I'll let you know. And sorry I haven't been good about writing." Ann's eyes watered. "I miss you guys a lot!"

"We miss you, too." Bob kissed her on the top of her head. "Bye, Annie." He and Nell waved as they proceeded out the main entrance.

Ann took a tissue from her purse and dabbed away her tears, trying not to smudge her mascara. Without warning, she heard footsteps approaching from behind.

She turned around with a start, the Kleenex balled up in her fist.

"Hi, Ann. Sorry, I didn't mean to startle you," Tim said, a look of embarrassment creeping across his face. "You mentioned last Wednesday that I should come to graduation." He held out a large mixed flower bouquet. "Here, these are for you. Congratulations."

Ann's lungs inflated like a party balloon.

"Tim! Wow ... um ... I didn't think you'd come." She shoved the tissue into her jacket pocket and grabbed hold of the bouquet, her thoughts aflutter. "The flowers are beautiful. Thank you."

"Sure." Tim shifted his weight from one leg to the other. "And would you like to go out for dinner soon at Del's Diner with me? He serves more than burgers and fries."

"Yes ... I'd like that."

Ann found herself twisting a long daisy leaf back and forth between her fingertips and stopped, dropping her free arm to her side.

"My phone number's in the phone book under Fred Castle. I'm staying at my parents' until I find something else."

Tim nodded and brushed his hand against her shoulder.

"See you soon, Ann."

"Um ... before you go, I'd ... like to ask you something." She hesitated, shifting her weight from one leg to the other. "Would you mind calling me Annie? If that's not too weird, that is."

"Sure, that's not weird at all. I like the ring to it, Annie." The corners of her eyes crinkled as she smiled. "Bye, Tim, and ... thanks again for the pretty flowers."

"My pleasure," he replied with a wave. "See you soon."

Ann watched as he walked through the door, her stomach leaping and lurching about as he glanced back at her. She turned around. *Okay, for goodness' sake, keep yourself together. Pretend you possess that 'confidence' Yvonne yammers about.*

Chapter Twelve

February – April 1977

Now, nine months after Tim had approached Ann at her high school graduation, it'd take more than dynamite to separate them, supplying Clifton's small-town busybodies with good reason to gossip. According to Yvonne's mother, those in her checkout line at the supermarket caught the prediction of rumormonger Ada Culpepper, a Southern transplant, when she said, "Oh, Lordy, y'all! Them two youngins is a weddin' jussa waitin' ta happen!"

If not dining out at Del's Diner or splitting a bucket of buttered popcorn at the Reel Theater, the pair could be found tearing up the bowling lanes in Silvermile.

Occasionally, the couple chose to spend the evening at Tim's bachelor pad, where he pulled on his imaginary chef's hat and prepared meals the likes of which even Mabel would have been proud. Ann, who once preferred the smell of horse manure to the aroma of horseradish or time spent in the kitchen, now lent a hand with the slicing, dicing, and peeling. Cleanup turned into a mutual chore.

Valentine's Day had arrived. As Ann blew out the last heart-shaped candle she'd bought on her way to Tim's apartment, he scraped leftover sautéed asparagus onto the serving platter next to what remained of the prime rib. He placed his wadded-up napkin on his plate and shot up from the table. Ann followed.

"No, sit still! I've made your favorite dessert—fudge brownie à la mode." Tim headed to the kitchen, pausing long enough in the doorway to catch her glance. "Hey, since it's our first Valentine's Day together, I figured we'd better really celebrate." He chuckled. "I even tossed extra chocolate chunks into the batter."

"No way! What have I done to deserve such royal treatment?"

Unknowingly drawing on the same Groucho Marx persona Ann's uncle Bob had used in his Great Roberto performance years ago, Tim said, "Hold that thought, m'dear!" And with a quirky side kick in midair, he disappeared.

Ann put on a broad grin and rolled her eyes. She said in a loud voice, "You and Uncle Bob are two of a kind! And I couldn't ask for more than that!" By the time she'd finished moving the dirty dinner dishes to the far side of the table, the clattering in the kitchen had stopped, and Tim reappeared with her à la mode. Ann noticed the heart-shaped sugar cookie with red iced lettering that Tim had pushed into the vanilla ice cream.

"You didn't make the cookie, too, did you?"

"No ... only embellished the top," Tim replied with the same quick head nod and crooked smile that made Ann's stomach do summersaults.

"What are you talking about? Bring the cookie closer, so I can see it." Her voice rose an octave. "Come on!"

"I will, but first, you asked me a minute ago what you've done to deserve such royal treatment, remember?"

"Yeah ... of course."

"Well, if you read the cookie and say *yes*, I'll promise you a lifetime of royal treatment!"

She cocked her head to one side. "What are you saying, Tim?"

Her breathing became rapid and shallow, and her insides did another flip flop.

"Here!" He set the bowl in front of Ann and rested his hands on her shoulders.

Leaning closer, she read the block letters aloud, oblivious to the fact that the word 'me' and the question mark that followed it hugged the cookie's edge. "Will you marry me?"

A shrill, high-pitched shriek blasted through the tiny dining room.

Ann catapulted out of the chair, turning to Tim so quickly that she pushed the corner of the chair away and knocked him backward.

"Oh, yes!" She wrapped her arms around his waist and rocked him back and forth like a wind-whipped tree limb, her adrenaline surging.

As Ann loosened her grip, Tim pulled a ring box from the front pocket of his tan corduroys. "It's the ring you said you liked in the jewelers' front window." He pulled the lid open. "It's not a big diamond, but will you wear it anyway?"

"Oh, Tim, yes! It's perfect!"

He plucked the engagement ring out of the box. "Here, let me put it on your finger so it'll be official." It easily slid on. "Oh, good, I'm glad I ordered the size 4½. I had doubts when it wouldn't slide over my pinky."

Ann sashayed over to the couch, yanked her Kodak Instamatic out of her purse, and checked the flashcube. "Take a picture of the ring and the cookie, will you please?" She handed the camera to Tim and extended her long, thin fingers toward the cookie, admiring the sparkle as the round diamond caught the overhead light. "And now, you need to help me eat your yummy creation before the ice cream melts."

Tim shot the pictures, and the young couple sat down, both high on excitement. "I can't wait to tell Sarah and Yvonne and, of course, Uncle Bob and Aunt Nell. And I'll run by the high school and tell Mrs. Tucker! I know she'll be happy for us."

"Well, believe it or not, your parents seemed okay with my

asking." Tim let out a hearty laugh. "Although, I think your mom still sees me as a *bag boy!*" He noticed the scrunched-up look of confusion on Ann's face. "Oh ... I stopped by your house last week when you were at work to ask your dad for your hand in marriage. Old fashioned, huh?"

Ann dropped her spoon into the bowl with a loud *ping*.

"That's one of the things I like best about you, Tim Palmer."

The abrupt realization that she'd one day soon be a Palmer brought forth another high-pitched shriek.

■ ■ ■

The couple decided on Saturday, September 18, as their tentative wedding date.

By choosing a date near the middle of the month, the two hoped that the cottonwood and aspen trees would still be waving their brilliant fall foliage.

Ann accepted Mabel's offer to make the wedding dress, although she knew it would involve concessions on her part. Soon, she'd accompany her mother to JC Penney in Silvermile to pick out a Simplicity pattern and look for suitable fabric. Mother and daughter agreed that the date called for an autumn theme.

By mid-April, Mabel insisted that Ann schedule an appointment with Dr. Wyatt, the Castle family physician at Clifton's sole clinic, for her first pelvic and breast examinations, the mandatory pre-marital blood test, and an opportunity to discuss future birth control options. Ann—grateful for the extra attention from her mother—hurriedly obliged.

Ann made an early-morning appointment for the following week. In the meantime, she arranged to go in to work at the newspaper an hour later than usual.

When the day arrived, her stomach felt queasy. She decided to skip breakfast and head to the clinic even though it might mean sitting inside Bubba and reading her tattered library copy of *Love Story* until time for her appointment.

As Ann steered into a parking spot in front of the gray-stucco clinic, she experienced a strong wave of nausea and vomited up a small amount of clear liquid into a heavy-duty plastic trash bag she kept on the driver's side window crank.

She wiped her mouth and fingers clean with a moist towelette from a pack in the glove box and dug through her purse for a cinnamon Tic Tac.

At last, she spotted the receptionist hang the 'open' sign on the front door.

Since Dr. Wyatt's first appointment failed to show up, a nurse's aide immediately ushered Ann into an examination room.

Once seated, the aide took her vital signs while giving her basic instructions on how to wear the cotton examination gown and thin paper drape that she handed her before leaving the room.

After arranging her new pantsuit over the back of a hard-plastic chair, Ann fumbled with the ties on the gown, giving her little time to get situated on the exam table before the doctor's sudden knock. She jumped at the sound and pushed the paper sheet against her lap, fearing her skin might appear as anemic white as the paper.

"Come in, Dr. Wyatt," she said, voice nearly inaudible.

Ann took a deep breath. *Yvonne said her first pelvic wasn't too bad. Now get a grip!* She listened as the doctor removed her file from the clear plastic holder outside the room.

Slowly, the door opened, and the dignified, white-haired physician entered, his Momma Cass lookalike nurse all but stepping on his heels. She closed the door and set about readying the doctor's equipment. The heavy, unexpected smell of antiseptic made Ann queasy. She swallowed hard and prayed she wouldn't throw up.

"Good morning, Ann; it's a pleasure to see you," Dr. Wyatt said in his usual warm, sincere manner. "And you remember my nurse, Mrs. Samuels?"

Mrs. Samuels looked up from the shallow metal cabinet drawer, chubby face beaming. "Hello, young lady! Happy spring!"

"Same to you." Ann quickly stilled her restless hands and folded them, worried that she was acting more like a middle schooler than the adult she'd supposedly become.

Dr. Wyatt continued, soft blue eyes locked on Ann's face, "It looks like you're here today for your first pelvic examination."

"Yes," Ann answered, eyes fixed on her knees. "I'm getting married in September."

"Well, congratulations, young lady!" replied Dr. Wyatt. "Who, may I ask, is the lucky fellow?"

Ann sat up straighter, a flicker of a smile replacing grim lips. She looked at the doctor. "Tim Palmer. He said you delivered him when he was a baby."

"Yes, I did, indeed. Saw him through his childhood illnesses, vaccinations ... all the regular stuff."

"And he told me you were very supportive when his mother passed away."

Dr. Wyatt nodded. "Tim's a fine man."

At that moment, he rubbed his slender hands together and changed the course of conversation. "Now, Ann, it looks like Nurse Samuels has everything all set up and ready for me to begin." He sat down on the metal rolling stool in front of the exam table and slipped on a pair of latex gloves while explaining each step of the procedures.

Ann's face grew as ruddy as a bushel of beets as the nurse

guided her feet into the stirrups and directed her to slide down to the edge of the table. "Okay, take a deep breath and relax. Dr. Wyatt will take over from here."

Seemingly determined to put her young patient at ease, Mrs. Samuels took her usual place at the doctor's side and asked Ann about the wedding plans in her smooth, alto voice. Minutes later, the doctor finished the pelvic exam and pulled off his gloves. Ann's face brightened.

Yvonne was right—this part of the exam went okay. It's not like Dr. Wyatt's never seen lady parts before.

"Good job," Nurse Samuels said. "You're a real trooper. I promise the breast exam will go much faster."

She moved back to the doctor's left side and watched as he completed this last step of the full examination, showing Ann how to give herself a monthly breast exam at home.

"Okay, sugar," said Mrs. Samuels, "it's time I move on to the next patient."

She gave Ann an arm pat. "You take good care of yourself. And again, congratulations!" At once, she took the sealed sample from a stainless-steel tray, opening the door wide enough to accommodate her ample girth.

Dr. Wyatt moved his stool to the front of the drop-down desktop and took a seat.

He opened her chart and thumbed through his notes from her last visit. "All right, Ann, it looks like you were scheduled for an appointment with Dr. Vargas at the Thurman Orthopedic Clinic in Denver back on April 21 of this year to discuss treatment for the curvature of your spine—kyphosis, as it's called. How did that go?"

Ann scooted back a few inches on the table and sat up straighter.

"Well, Dr. Wyatt, like you said during my last appointment, a curvature like mine at my age is irreversible without surgery. And

Dr. Vargas said the surgery's risky." She adjusted the paper drape, smoothing out the wrinkles. "He also believes that the kyphosis was caused by a birth defect. He said that if I would've seen a specialist when I was younger, I could've been fitted for a back brace, eliminating the need for surgery. Unfortunately, the pediatrician my mother took me to see said the curvature was *psychosomatic* and would disappear as I developed more self-confidence. He compared me to a shy turtle pulling its head into its shell."

After which, Mother took perverse delight in calling me Turtle. Turtles, once delightful creatures, became God's greatest design disaster.

Ann's whole body shook.

"Anyway, despite the kyphosis, Dr. Vargas was pleased by how limber I am."

Dr. Wyatt dipped his head in agreement.

"I look forward to receiving his report. Anything else?"

"That I should be thankful I'm not experiencing the fatigue and back pain many sufferers do." Stilling her legs from swinging, she added, "He also gave me exercise handouts to strengthen the muscles in my upper back and suggested I consider physical therapy."

"That sounds like a terrific suggestion. I'll write you a script for the physical therapy. There're several good therapists in Silvermile." Dr. Wyatt closed Ann's chart, folded his hands in his lap, and looked into her eyes. "Now, young lady, I have a few tough questions to ask you."

Ann's face ignited into flames, and her muscles grew tense.

"Okay," she replied, voice shaky.

"When was your last period?"

She adjusted her position, grabbing the sides of the exam table and gulping for air. "Oh, my … well, maybe … gosh. I'm not sure. Maybe five or six weeks ago? I forget. I'm sorry."

"Could you be pregnant, Ann? Your pelvic exam indicates that you might be."

Her mouth became dry, and she feared she might go deaf from the pounding in her ears. She summoned her voice for any sound at all. "Yes ... I guess ... I could be."

Oh, gawd! Slow down, heart! Please!

"All right, Ann. We'll need to test a urine sample to be certain. There're containers and instructions on the shelf in the bathroom above the toilet. When you're finished, take the container to the lab across the hall. They'll also draw blood for your pre-marital blood test." Dr. Wyatt stood and walked to the door, Ann's chart tucked under his arm.

He stopped and looked over his shoulder. "After they're done with you in the lab, come back to the exam room. I'll return when I receive the results."

"Thank you," Ann replied, head hung low.

The door closed. "Oh, Lord! Mother's going to kill me! She'll hold this against me for the rest of her life."

With rigid, robotic motions, she changed back into her pantsuit and followed the doctor's instructions.

The minutes of waiting for the results seemed to drag into months, every *tick-tock* of the plastic wall clock making her flinch.

Ann's thoughts whirled inside her skull with such force that she grabbed onto the sides of the exam table for support. She closed her eyes and saw her mother in stereoscopic vision on the backs of her eyelids, towering above her in a bulky black judge's robe as she cowered underneath a massive wooden table. *"Guilty!"* Mabel said, banging an enormous gavel against the tabletop.

"You're guilty of being irresponsible and stupid! Ann Marie, you're such an embarrassment! You always have been and always will be!"

THE BROKEN TURTLE BLUES

Startled and shaken, a rap on the door brought Ann back to the room. She fumbled to wipe the perspiration off her upper lip. "Come in."

Dr. Wyatt sat on the stool and opened Ann's chart. "Yes, it's as I thought, you're pregnant." He looked into her eyes as they pooled. "I know this must be difficult. Please ask me any questions that come to mind."

A rush of heat skyrocketed through her blood vessels. She slowly bobbed her head, afraid to move too hastily for fear the floodgates would open further and a torrent of tears would break loose.

"Ann, let's come up with a due date. Do you have any idea when you might have become pregnant?"

Dr. Wyatt's calculations pinpointed Ann's pregnancy at six weeks, the due date set for November 11.

He wrote a prescription for prenatal vitamins and instructed her to make another appointment with the receptionist for the first week in June.

Embarrassed and desperate for a breath of fresh air, Ann rose from the table and followed the doctor out of the examination room. She waited in the hallway until he disappeared around the corner before racing full throttle past the receptionist's desk and out the front door, not once looking past her feet, avoiding eye contact.

In less than five minutes, Ann nosed Bubba into a tight parking space near the back door of All Foods Market. Several employees spotted her through the break room window, which overlooked the south end of the parking lot, and waved through the ghost-white tendrils of cigarette smoke that encircled their heads.

Ann entered the back of the cinder-block building and peeked into the cluttered break room through its open doorway.

Peggy, the market's bookkeeper, waved. "Hi, Annie, you must have the day off. Tim's in his office."

"Thanks, Peggy. I won't be but a minute," she replied, feeling an urgent longing to cough out the second-hand smoke from her lungs.

Tim's office door appeared ajar. Ann knocked.

"It's open. Come in."

Ann peeked around the edge of the door. "Hey, it's me."

Tim looked at his watch and frowned. "Weren't you supposed to be back to work by now? Was there a hang-up at the doctor's office?"

"You could say that." Ann entered the office, closing the door. Her face twisted like a corkscrew, bottom lip quivering.

She staggered over to his desk.

Tim rose from his chair and pulled her into an embrace. "What's going on?"

Sobbing into his chest, Ann answered, "I'm six weeks pregnant. I thought I threw up this morning because I was nervous about my appointment, but maybe it was morning sickness. I don't know." She peeled herself away from his comforting hold and stepped back. "But I do know Mother and Dad are going to kill me! And what about your dad, Tim?" All of a sudden, she closed her fist and smacked herself repeatedly on the forehead.

Tim grabbed her by both wrists.

"Hey, stop that! What the hell are you doing?"

He pulled her closer. Silence stood between them like a dark stranger.

"All right, look ... this is a huge shock, and of course, we should've been more careful. But it's also pretty exciting. Huh?"

He let go of her wrists and cradled her face in his hands.

"All that matters, Annie, is that this baby is going to have two loving parents. The grandparents will come around. I guarantee it."

"How can you be so all-fired sure, Tim?"

"I've never told you this before ... probably because the subject's never come up, but I was conceived out of wedlock. And to the best of my knowledge, everyone survived the initial shock just fine."

Ann tilted her head back, searching his wise, soulful eyes, and nodded.

"Okay, we'll see."

■ ■ ■

Several days passed. Since Ann refused to advertise their predicament by parading down the aisle with a well-rounded *basketball*, the couple decided against a September wedding. And right or wrong, she persuaded Tim that they should wait until after the ceremony to tell even the immediate family about the baby.

As luck would have it, Tim's favorite aunt—his late mother's widowed sister—had recently signed a contract on a small cottage in a retirement community in San Diego and planned to make the move from Clifton at the end of June.

Tim saw his aunt Betty's pending relocation as an opportunity to push the wedding ceremony up to the first part of June to ensure her valued participation in the wedding.

To the couple's surprise, First Presbyterian, the Castle's home church, had no events scheduled for the afternoon of June 4. So without hesitation, Ann booked their wedding for that day. Thoughts of Sammy and Yvonne popped into her mind.

She hoped her two best friends' summertime plans wouldn't keep them from serving as bridesmaids.

First, though, she dialed her mother and dad from her desk at the newspaper office and arranged to bring Tim by the house at six o'clock that evening to discuss the new wedding date. At the least, she figured her mother would appreciate the fact that an earlier wedding date would mean a sooner move-out date.

Tim immediately contacted his father and was pleased that he and Aunt Betty insisted on lending a hand with the cost and preparation of the food for the reception. He planned to tell Ann and her parents the good news that evening.

Ann wheeled Bubba into the employee parking section at All Foods Market ten minutes before their pre-arranged time. She cupped her hand above her eyeglass frames and watched the brilliant flaming-orange sun as it disappeared behind the mountain peaks, taking the day's mild temperature with it.

Chilled, she pulled on her windbreaker and cranked up the driver's side window.

After a quick glance in all directions to check for unwelcome stares, Ann placed her hand on her small belly, closed her eyes, and spoke out loud to the baby. "Hello, little one. This is your mommy talking. Do you know you've made me the luckiest mommy in the world? I don't know what I've done to deserve you. I'm—" She stopped talking. *Whoa!*

Out of the blue, Ann had become a five-year-old again, lying limp on her mother's lap in the old family rocker. Sick with the flu, she listened as Mabel sang and cooed to her and her life-sized baby doll—the one with soft brown curls and pink plaid pajamas undoubtedly stuffed in a box somewhere in the garage.

She leaned back in the seat, caught up in her daydream.

I know you still have a soft side, Mother. I see it in the way you talk to poor old Zeek when he lies at your feet in the evening or the way you care for the chicks when they hatch. And each summer, for as long as I can remember, I've watched you give loving attention to your vegetable garden—weeding, watering, and treating the soil.

I crave your soft, nurturing side. Why can't you see that? Why do you keep it from me?

Ann pulled out a tissue from her coat pocket and blew her nose.

You and Dad have given me many nice material possessions over the years, and I appreciate that even though I haven't always shown it. But what I want ... no, what I need, is that 'soft you' and your acceptance of this innocent baby after the wedding's over. Please, is that even remotely possible?

Tim noticed that Ann appeared lost in thought. He leaned down beside the driver's side window, waving his hand. Ann sensed his presence, turning her head in his direction. He opened the door, and she nestled her face in the crook of his neck.

"Hey, Annie, ready to face the critics?"

Chapter Thirteen

November 1977

Tim leaned against the pale wall that flanked the double doors leading to Silvermile's hospital's Radiology Department and waited, his hands shoved deep inside the pockets of his jeans. Suddenly, he cringed, removing his hands and looking at his watch as Ann's stifled shrieks traveled through the closed doors and hit his eardrums, the contractions three minutes apart. As she quieted, he pushed his hands back inside his pockets and waited for the next series of contractions.

Dr. Wyatt soon appeared, pulling the foot of Ann's gurney through the doorway and out into the hall. He stopped to show Tim the X-ray, removing it from its large manila jacket and holding it up toward the florescent fixture suspended from the ceiling.

"Here, Tim," he said, pointing, "these are the baby's feet, and this is the birth canal."

"Uh-huh," Tim replied, adjusting his plastic-rimmed glasses and looking closely.

"Unfortunately, as I've discussed with Ann, this confirms that the baby is breech. This means that we're going to have to do a cesarean section. And since Ann's already signed the consent form, we'll take her into surgery now." The doctor slid the film back inside the envelope. "Do you have any questions?"

Tim cleared his throat, breaths quickening. "No, Dr. Wyatt, but I'd like to wish Annie well before you wheel her away."

By the time Tim walked around to the head of the narrow gurney, Ann had flipped onto her side once again, fighting another vicious contraction—everything practiced in Lamaze class forgotten. He placed his hand on the nape of her neck and whispered.
"Hey there, sweetie, I know this isn't how we planned for the birth to happen, but—"
"Gawd, it hurts, Tim! I need them to get *this thing* out, now!"
Tim grimaced and grinned sheepishly at Dr. Wyatt, his face lit up like the red 'exit' sign letters overhead.
"Go get a strong cup of coffee and something to eat, Tim," he said in a reassuring tone, the corners of his mouth turning up slightly. "I'll come out to the surgery waiting room when we're through."
Dr. Wyatt motioned to the orderly at the head of the gurney to proceed. Tim's shoulders dropped as he stepped back into the middle of the long hallway and listened to Ann's agonizing moans. He cupped his hands around his mouth. "I'll be waiting for you and our baby, Annie!"

■ ■ ■

Ann arrived at her vacant semi-private room in the Maternity Ward by eleven o'clock that night. Someone had left a plush stuffed elephant with a bright rainbow-striped ribbon propped up against the telephone on the bedside table.
"Hello, Mommy!" Tim said, slipping into the room. He leaned over the bed and kissed Ann on her forehead before smoothing several stray hairs around her center part. "How're you feeling?"
"Still a little groggy, Daddy-O. And it's driving me crazy that I can't move my legs. I don't know how long it takes for a spinal to wear off." Ann rubbed her palms back and forth across her thighs. "More importantly, though, how about our precious baby?"

Tim's whole body seemed to smile. "How can anything so small be so perfect?"

"I know." Ann took hold of his hand and squeezed. "I see somebody's been by already." She nodded toward the stuffed animal. "Who's the cute little elephant from?"

"My dad. He's out in the hallway in front of the nursery window, making a huge fuss over his beautiful new granddaughter. You ought to hear him. Not that many employees are here this late at night, but I bet he's stopping all those who walk by and asking them to take a peek at her!"

"He's going to make such a good grandpa." Ann looked Tim straight in the eyes. "And what about my parents? You called them, didn't you?"

"Of course, I did, sweetie. I called them right after you were taken into surgery. Your mom wanted to wait until she reached Sarah at her dorm room to tell her about the C-section before she and your dad—"

"Hello, you two," Fred said as he poked his head around the open door. "I know it's late, but the nurse at the front desk told me it was okay to stop by for a few minutes. Are you up for a visit, Ann Marie?"

"Sure, Dad," she replied, motioning him into the room, its seafoam green walls screaming 'hospital here!' "We were just talking about you."

Fred entered the room. "Mabel will be here in a minute. She's down at the nursery window with Al, hoping to get a picture of the baby. And before I forget, Sarah sends her love to all three of you." He walked over to Tim by the head of the bed and shook his hand, grabbing his shoulder with his free hand and drawing him close. "Congratulations, Tim. She's a keeper!"

"And hello there, daughter!" He removed his brown felt derby and walked around to the other side of the bed. "It's hard to believe you now have your own daughter!" He bent over the bedrail and kissed Ann on the cheek. "Did you decide on the name Katie May?"

"We did. And the name would've been Michael Raymond if she were a boy. Mike for short." Ann patted her father's hand. "I hope Mother's okay with us using Tim's mom's name for the first name instead of hers. It's such a nice tribute to her memory." She removed her hand from his and smoothed down the ends of the medical tape surrounding the IV needle in her wrist. "Although maybe we shouldn't have shortened Mabel to May for the middle name. Mother's probably not too happy about that either."

Actually, I'd hate to saddle a kid with the name Mabel for a multitude of reasons!

Fred leaned his forearms against the top rail.

"You know your mother, Ann Marie. She needs time to let things soak in. She'll come around." He pushed himself back to an upright position. "She's definitely excited about having a grandchild. Before long, I'll have to pry her away from the nursery window."

"I might need you to shoo my dad this way, too, Fred!" He picked up a yellowed plastic chair and set it down next to Fred. "In the meantime, please sit." Tim slid a second chair to the other side of the bed for himself. "Why do hospital rooms have to be so doggone cramped?"

A willowy nurse in a crisp white uniform and cap knocked and entered the room. She looked at Ann with the kind eyes and pleasant smile of many small-town folks. "Hello, Mrs. Palmer. My name's Sylvia. I'll be your nurse for the rest of the night."

"Please, call me Ann."

"All right, Ann it is."

"Thank you. And how's Katie, our baby?"

"She's in the nursery being quite vocal. Do you feel up to trying to breastfeed?"

Ann nodded. "Yes ... I think so ... I'd like to see her."

Fred rose from the chair and moved it to one side.

"Well, sorry to interrupt, but that's my cue to leave, Ann Marie. It's late anyway, and you're going to need your rest. We'll come back tomorrow. Okay?"

"Of course, Dad, thanks for coming!"

"Why don't I walk you to the nursery, Fred? It'll give me an opportunity to say hello to Mabel and walk Dad out to his car. He didn't get to see Annie, either, so he'll be coming back tomorrow as well." He winked at Ann. "I'll only be a few minutes."

Both men left the room. Sylvia pulled Ann higher up toward the head of the bed, unsnapped the back of the flimsy hospital gown, and helped her pull her free arm through the short sleeve. She covered Ann's exposed shoulder with a thin warming blanket and walked over to the opposite side of the bed.

"Here's a nifty little trick," Sylvia said, pulling the snaps apart on the underside of the second sleeve. "This way, we won't have to thread the IV bag through the sleeve." She pulled the rest of the cotton blanket over Ann's other shoulder. "Are you able to feel any tingling yet in your legs?"

"Yeah, maybe a little bit."

"Good. We'll want to give you Demerol for the pain before the spinal wears off. But let's try breastfeeding first. And after I return your baby to the nursery, I'll come back in here and inject a dose into your IV."

Like a tender mother, Sylvia patted Ann on the shoulder. "I'll be right back with the baby."

Ann rubbed her fingers along her dry, cracked lips, wishing she'd remembered to ask the nurse for the ChapStick tube Tim had laid out for her on the bedside table. She closed her eyes, mind drifting. *How bad will the pain be after the anesthesia wears off? And what happens if I can't get the hang of breastfeeding? Tim, hurry back in here!*

■ ■ ■

Early the next morning, Tim stood at the nurse's station waiting for a refill of ice chips for Ann when Dr. Wyatt rushed up to the desk and seized her chart. Tim caught his eyes, and the two men exchanged a nod.

Dr. Wyatt walked over to Tim, giving him a pat on the back. "I'm glad you're already here. I actually need to talk with you both this morning." He pointed to Ann's door. "Please, son, you lead the way."

"Is there something wrong, Dr. Wyatt?" he asked, looking over his shoulder, voice steeped in concern.

"Let's step into the room where we can talk in private."

Tim set the empty pitcher on Ann's bedside table and walked around to the far side of the bed.

"Hello, Ann," Dr. Wyatt said, scanning the Progress Notes in her chart. "How are you feeling?"

"Sore, but the pain medicine helps."

"Good. Be certain to ask for it before the pain gets too bad. You don't want it to get ahead of you."

Ann bobbed her head. "I will."

"All right," Dr. Wyatt resumed, looking again at her chart, "the nurses report that you're consistently doing your coughing and deep breathing every few hours and that your incision looks good. That means we'll plan on getting you up out of bed today." He set the open chart on the bedside table and wrote the day's orders. "I'll also order a liquid diet for your lunchtime meal and have the nurse remove your catheter this afternoon." Snapping the chart closed, the doctor looked at the first-time parents, compassion in his eyes.

"Ann and Tim, while I don't want to alarm you, I'm afraid Katie's having difficulty breathing this morning."

Ann clutched Tim's hand. "Oh, no, what's wrong with her?"

"Katie has a disorder called hyaline membrane disease. It's a condition in which an infant's lungs are initially deficient in a material called surfactant, which is necessary to help the lungs inflate and deflate properly throughout the normal breathing cycle."

He stroked his long chin. "Now, this usually occurs in premature infants, but since she was delivered within a couple days of the due date and is of a good birth weight, I imagine the eight-thousand-foot altitude here in the valley has played a part in the surfactant deficiency and, thus, in her difficulty getting the air she needs."

Tim leaned forward. "What's being done to help her?"

"She's receiving oxygen, but she's going to need treatment that we're not equipped to give her here. I've been in contact with Dr. Peter Jacobs of the Neonatal Intensive Care Unit at Denver Children's Hospital, where they have all the equipment and treatments she'll need. He can have a helicopter on its way in twenty minutes. I just need your signatures."

"Yes, of course," Ann said, eyes darting between the two men.

Tim dipped his head in agreement. "Certainly."

"Okay, I'm going to make a few phone calls so we can get this ball rolling."

Ann's heart pounded. "May we see her before she goes?"

"Yes, I'll make certain her bassinet's wheeled in here," Dr. Wyatt replied as he darted out the door. He abruptly spun around and looked back at the devastated couple. "This is treatable. And keep in mind that she's one tough cookie ... like her mother."

■ ■ ■

Tim jumped up from the chair and tackled the black push-button phone on the first ring, pulling so hard on the heavy plastic receiver that he hit himself in the chest with it. He fumbled to get the receiver to his mouth.

"Hello ... yes, this is Tim Palmer. Yes, Dr. Jacobs ... she *did*?"

Ann batted at Tim's arm but missed. She struggled to move her lips, rational thoughts levitating beyond reach. "Tim!" she said, speech slurred. "Tim! Did you say she *died*? Answer me!"

Tim covered the mouthpiece with his palm.

"No, Annie, this is Dr. Jacobs. He called to tell us that Katie's arrived at Children's. I'll finish talking to him, and then I'll fill you in."

"Oh, *good*!" she replied, drifting off into another drug-induced blur.

"I'm sorry, Dr. Jacobs. The nurse gave my wife some pain medication a while ago, and I'm afraid she's a bit loopy. Yes ... okay, that's great news. Thanks again."

Tim hung up the phone and massaged his temples.

"Thank you, God," he said in a whisper, glancing toward the acoustic-tiled ceiling. He straddled the chair and slid it next to Ann's bed, his knees spread wide apart, touching the mattress. Watching her sleep, he succumbed to a deep yawn, folding his arms next to her hip and laying his head down. Moments later, the couple's slow, even breaths filled the room.

■ ■ ■

Ann finished the lukewarm chicken broth and droopy Jell-O squares before removing her tea from the dinner tray for later and pushing the rickety over-bed table off to the side.

The post-surgical gas pains that earlier bored through her intestines like an auger had subsided since her first walk down the hallway.

After adjusting the bed, Ann shut her eyes and recounted the last conversation Tim had had with a neonatal nurse at Children's Hospital before he'd left for home.

Katie's faring well on the respirator, her vitals are strong and stable, and she's reacting favorably to treatment.

A brisk knock on the door disrupted Ann's thoughts. "Come in."

Mabel pushed the door open wide enough to poke her head through the opening.

"Hello, Ann Marie. Your father has a county zoning meeting this evening at the courthouse, so I had him drop me off."

Ann's breath caught in her throat, and her muscles tightened.

She mustered enough energy to hide her distress behind an ample grin, wishing she could trade her mother's visit for those rip-roaring gas pains again. "Come in, Mother. There're hooks on the back of the door if you'd like to hang up your coat."

Pointing to the stack of chairs underneath the wall-mounted television, she added, "And you can bring a chair over here by the bed."

"No," Mabel replied, taking hold of the chair on the top, "I'll slide it over here in the corner away from that drafty doorway, and I'll keep my coat on, too. Your room's downright cold."

"Okay." *Although I bet the 'draft,' real or imagined, came from your frosty presence, Mother.* Ann craned her neck toward the corner. "I can barely see you over there."

"That's fine," Mabel said, voice flat. "Just turn on the television. We can talk later."

Ann didn't answer.

Can't even ask me how I'm holding up, huh? Of course, why should this be any different than the whole damn pregnancy? You never asked me how I was doing then either. Well ... so much for seeing that freakin' 'soft side' of you again! Fine! Screw you!

She pushed down hard on the red TV 'power' button, firing through the limited number of available channels and settling on the ABC Evening News.

Ann's poor long-distance vision made Harry Reasoner's grainy close-up even more blurry. Her tortoiseshell specs sat out of reach on the far side of the over-bed table. But rather than ask Mabel for help, Ann squinted at the television and leaned farther forward, tugging on her incision and causing her to wince.

Conceding to the impossible, she eased back into the mattress.

Without her glasses, Reasoner's fuzzy facial features and white helmet of hair substituted nicely for Uncle Bob's. A sudden urge to call her uncle a second time yanked at her heart, but like her glasses, the phone sat out of reach.

Exasperated, Ann lowered the head of the bed, pulled the thin sheet over her mouth, and shut her eyes.

Maybe if I pretend to fall asleep with the TV on, she'll leave. I should be so lucky. She took slow, even breaths—one after another.

■ ■ ■

Ann drew her wrist close to her face, twisting her loosely clasped watchband until the numbers faced upright. Enough light spilled into her hospital room through the doorway for her to make out the time.

"Wow, it can't be one-thirty in the morning!"

Still sprawled out on her back, Ann craned her neck to the side, glancing at her mother's vacant chair. She grimaced as she repositioned her sore hips, her thoughts turning to Katie.

Hey, little one, I hope you feel the love I'm sending your way. I know in my heart that you're going to be fine.

"It's your damn grandma I wonder about. Ugh!"

What was with her tonight? It's the first time she's come into my room, and she didn't say more than a dozen words to me. She can volunteer to chat with nursing home residents yet can't muster up the friendliness of a stranger with her daughter.

Is this her weird way of coping with your illness, Katie?

Or is she still disappointed that I was pregnant before the wedding?

No ... forget disappointed ... try infuriated! Well, I'm fed up with her sulky behavior!

Ann pulled the skinny pillow over her face and muffled sob after deep sob until exhaustion robbed her strength.

Chapter Fourteen

July 1986

Katie hollered up the second set of steps from her perch on the landing. "Mom, where are you?" She glanced at her Funtime Barbie watch, seemingly pleased that she'd mastered the task of telling the time.

"We're late! I told Grammy you'd drop me off at ten o'clock!"

"All right, Katie! I hear you!" Ann struggled to secure the clasp on her necklace while darting out of the master bedroom. "Don't forget to grab the sack of PB&J sandwiches and put it in your backpack. It's on the bottom shelf of the fridge."

"Okay," Katie replied, scurrying into the kitchen.

She opened the refrigerator door, removed the brown paper bag, and took a quick survey of the other shelves, mouth gaping open.

Ann snuck up behind her. "Boo!"

Katie stepped back, rolling her eyes. "Good try, Mom, but you didn't scare me."

A sunny smile stretched across Ann's face. "Yeah, I think I did a teeny bit!"

"Nuh-uh! Not until you stop wearing your flip-flops. They always make that wacky sound. Hey, can I have a few tangelos?"

"I don't know, *can* you?" Ann asked in jest.

Katie huffed, but a slight smile gave away her pretense.

"The answer's yes ... you *may* have a few tangelos. If you learn that handy-dandy grammar rule, Katydid, you'll be every teacher's pet!"

"Haha, Mom! You're the only one who cares about that grammar junk."

Counting out six of the largest tangelos, she put three in each pocket of her bright-purple windbreaker.

"Do you want to take a pair of old jeans in case you and Grammy play in the meadow?"

"I already grabbed 'em. They're in my backpack. And I'm taking my camera." Katie raced over to the entryway table and picked up the nylon backpack Aunt Sarah had bought her at the local five-and-dime store, solely because the color matched Katie's windbreaker.

"Why don't you toss the tangelos in your pack, too, so they don't fall out of your pockets?"

"All right." Katie unzipped the side pocket and stuffed them inside. "Now, can we go?" she asked, tapping her foot on the floor.

"Yes, I'm ready. The van's unlocked."

By the time Ann pulled the front door shut, Katie had already fastened her seatbelt. She motioned through the windshield for Ann to hurry.

That little poop! Ann chuckled, tying the loose ends of her short-sleeve blouse into a knot. She marveled that her tank top underneath it matched the burnt-orange color of the tangelos. Shielding her eyes from the sun, she scanned the cloudless span of cerulean sky. Late spring into early summer remained her favorite time of the year. The birds' cheerful songs, the lilac bushes' luscious, sweet fragrance, the animal babies' playful antics, and the sun's toasty warmth as it seeped into her bones all filled her with joy.

Ann parked the white Dodge Caravan in front of her parents'

house next to Bubba and turned off the ignition, stilling the plastic bauble on the end of the keyring from swinging back and forth.

"Who named Bubba, Mom? Was it Grandpa Fred or Grammy?" Ann looked at her inquisitive eight-year-old. "Well, the credit for that one goes to me!"

Katie giggled. "It's a pretty silly name, Mom!"

"Oh, it's even worse than that. Are you ready to hear Bubba's full name?"

"Yes!" Katie bobbed her head, toffee-brown eyes as bright as a 100-watt bulb.

Leaning forward, she drummed her hands across the dashboard.

"Hold onto your socks, Katie, because here it comes!" Ann conjured up a deep voice. "Bubba's full name is Bubba the Beast!"

The drumming stopped, and Katie snorted. "Oh, my gosh, that's stupid!"

"Yep, I told you so." Out of the corner of her eye, Ann spotted her father in a bright-yellow T-shirt coming toward them from the barnyard. "Here comes Grandpa Fred. He must have been out at the barn checking on the horses. Ready to grab your stuff?"

"Yes, yahoo!" Katie snatched her backpack and opened the van door. Before getting out, she looked at her mom. "Next time you drop me off, will you stay and watch me ride Lucky again?"

"Sure. The poor old fella. We should do that more often."

Fred opened the driver's door and stepped back with an inviting grin. "Hello, you two!"

Katie jumped out the passenger door and rushed over to give him a hug. "I made us PB&J sandwiches, Grandpa Fred. I hope Grammy has potato chips to go with 'em! Oh, and I also brought tangelos," she added, her words charging his ears as she disappeared through the door to the house.

"Don't you wish you could bottle her energy, Dad?"

Nodding, Fred answered, "Yes ... but it'd take more than a few spoonfuls for me these days."

"Me, too." She pretended to yawn. "Isn't it nap time yet?"

Fred cracked a slight smile, a few moments of awkward silence passing between them.

"Well, I suppose I'll take off. I need to run a few errands before I go work at the church."

"First, would you take a moment to say hello to your mother?"

Ann's body grew stiff and motionless like the brownish-gray coyote on display in the front window of Pete's Taxidermy. She swallowed hard and struggled to inhale.

Why can't you stop insisting I say hello? You've got to know your brooding troll-wife hates my guts!

The urge to slam the van door shut and back out the gateway grabbed at her chest, but the nagging obligation of mustering to duty like the good little soldier of her youth took charge. "All right, Dad," she answered, trying to squelch the trepidation in her voice.

Fred led the way to the kitchen.

Mabel held a large bag of Lay's potato chips open for Katie, who'd already stuffed a handful into the first of three sandwich baggies laid out across the cluttered countertop.

"Hang on a minute, you two ... look at who else is here!" Grandmother and granddaughter abruptly turned toward Ann.

"Hi, Mother," Ann said, voice stiff. "I want to wish you and Katie a fun day." She pointed to the bright kitchen window, still framed by the same dingy blue-and-white gingham curtains that had come with the house. "You couldn't ask for a nicer day to go out and play."

Mabel urged Katie to fill the last two plastic baggies while Ann looked on. When filled, she slowly folded the slick yellow top of the Lay's bag and secured it with a wooden clothespin before asking Fred to put it back on the top of the refrigerator.

"Well, Ann Marie," Mabel said through a half-smile, "it might make for a nicer day if you wouldn't rush off like you always do." She stepped closer to Ann, and with the crossed arms of a general, she lowered her voice. "You're not running off to talk to your new counselor about me, are you?"

Ann clasped her hands behind her back and squeezed, anger roiling beneath her skin.

She'd discussed the counselor with Fred in confidence.

Why did nothing between her father and her remain private? She locked and loaded on her mother's smug look of one-upmanship. "Nope, not today."

"Fine," Mabel replied.

She turned on her heel and stepped over to the sink, her back toward the others.

A flaming-red scowl unfolded across Katie's forehead.

Ann pulled her daughter to her chest. "Have fun with Grammy and Grandpa Fred, okay? And remember, I love you more than all the pecan pies in the world!"

Katie stepped back and looked into her mom's eyes, now soft. Bobbing her head, she gave a thumbs-up. "I love you, too!" She giggled. "Mom, you said *hey* ... and *hay* is for horses! Remember?"

Ann winked at Katie before glancing at her father.

"I'll be back around four o'clock ... call me at the church if you need me to come earlier." She headed to the van without saying goodbye.

"Why do I let those two push my buttons?" *And why can't I remember to take the deep, cleansing breaths I learned in counseling?*

Dad, you're such an enabler. And where would I even begin with you, Mother?

■ ■ ■

By quarter to two, the other volunteers had left the church. Ann stood on a metal folding chair, stapling the last of the whimsical animal border across the top of the bulletin board in the narthex. She stepped down and stood back, taking one last look at their collaborative effort. Satisfied, she put the chair and stapler away and locked the back door behind her. With time left before she needed to pick up Katie, Ann decided to drink in the delicious weather by driving over to Sunset Hill and walking the cemetery's perimeter.

The gravel parking area adjacent to the newest section of cemetery plots had emptied. Ann pushed her purse under the driver's seat and changed into the sneakers she kept in a plastic crate in the far back.

Rivulets of water ran perpendicular to the gravel pathway, signaling the completion of the day's watering cycle. Ann cheered since dodging the stray mist from the sprinklers annoyed her. She looked at her watch and counted forward thirty minutes. *Okay, I need to keep moving till at least 3:42.*

She breathed deeply and set off at a fast pace, vigorously pumping her arms.

As Ann settled into a comfortable rhythm, she reminisced about past cemetery encounters, beginning with the jitters Sarah and she had felt on their first trip to Clifton when they realized their soon-to-be neighbors *existed* under the ground.

Frame by frame, she replayed the times she'd coaxed high school friends into rebellious behavior, unbeknownst to her parents: the night she and Yvonne dressed as ghosts in her mother's good sheets; her moonlit midnight tour through the oldest section with the crooked, crumbling headstones; and the time she'd dared classmate Glenn Douglas to jump in and out of a newly dug grave visible to oncoming cars on Steele Street. She chuckled at her mischievousness.

Right ... and I thought I was such a goody-two-shoes!

On her fourth trip around the cemetery's perimeter, Ann glanced across the street and spotted Katie and Mabel in the meadow, playing on a fallen Cottonwood tree that had long ago become their 'rocket ship to the moon.'

She watched out the corner of her eye as pilot and co-pilot straddled the widest part of the trunk, rocking back and forth in sync as if accelerating at great speed.

You're quite the pair, you two! And you, Mommy dearest... you suck at being a mother, but for some inexplicable reason, you're a good grandmother. I'll give you that much. Who'd have guessed you'd take to her so fast?

Dad told me you were glued to the nursery window that first night at the hospital.

It was me you didn't want anything to do with.

You blamed me for her hyaline membrane disease ... like you blamed me for Sarah's broken arm when we were kids, and like you still blame me for my freakin' turtle-shell back. Anyway, please don't toss her aside when you're no longer the center of her universe.

All of a sudden, Ann heard Fred shouting her name.

She looked toward the front of the house as she continued walking and saw him waving her over. *Geez, Dad, I wasn't done.*

Ann pointed to the van and hollered, "I'll drive on over, Dad. Give me a minute."

She watched as he waved before disappearing into the house.

Picking up her pace, she moved straight for the van.

Without bothering to change out of her tennis shoes, Ann slid into the driver's seat. She took a swig of lukewarm water from the plastic water bottle nestled in the dashboard console, wiping her mouth with her hand. Dismissing her seatbelt, she pulled out onto Steele Street and drove the seventy-five yards before making a sharp left-hand turn into her parents' graveled driveway.

Fred held the front door open, his neutral expression out of character.

"Everything all right, Dad?"

"Come sit for a minute, Ann Marie," he said, pulling two chairs out from the dining room table. "I'm afraid I've got bad news."

"Huh?" Ann's crinkled brow grew pale.

He turned the farthest chair around and straddled it, patting the cushion on the other while brushing off a few dried crumbs. "Please, sit."

"Okay, but I don't think I want to hear this. My heart's pounding in my throat!"

Fred clasped his hands around hers and squeezed. "I'm afraid there's no easy way to say this, Ann Marie."

"What, Dad? Tell me!"

"Your uncle Bob was killed in a car accident this afternoon."

Ann broke free from her father's grip, tossed her eyeglasses on the tabletop, and buried her face inside her trembling hands.

"No! Oh, my gawd, I was afraid you were going to say something horrible like that! It's not true! It can't be!" She lowered her hands into her lap and looked at her father through tear-stained eyes, lips squeezed tight and chin quivering. "Have you talked to Aunt Nell yet?"

"No. She's pretty shook up. The hired hand called ... Sam something. He hasn't been working at the ranch too long. Unfortunately, he didn't know the details. I believe—"

Time stopped. Fred's words bounced off her eardrums and embedded themselves in the sludge encasing her brain. She slumped over and placed her forehead on the vinyl tablecloth, uncertain if day had yet faded into night.

The doorbell rang. Ann looked at her father with puffy red eyes, tears streaming down her sallow cheeks. "Please, Dad, I don't want anyone to see me like this."

Fred squeezed her shoulder and stood. "Don't worry, honey. I imagine it's Tim. While you were driving over here, I called him at the market to see if he'd leave early and pick you up." He moved his chair to one side and walked to the door.

Ann grabbed the napkin holder on the far side of the table and placed it in front of her. She pulled out several, wiping her face dry with the first and putting the others inside the front pocket of her jean shorts.

Tim came up behind her and kissed the top of her bowed head. "Hey, sweetie. I'm sorry about Uncle Bob."

"I know. Thank you." Ann twisted around in her seat so she could see Tim's face. "It's still hard to take it in. The thought of it makes me sick. And poor Aunt Nell; I can't imagine. I guess I'll wait and call her tomorrow."

"That's a good idea," Tim softly replied.

Ann felt one of the cats rub against her shin. She pushed the edge of the tablecloth to one side and spotted Sassy. "Come here, big guy ... this is the pits, isn't it?" she asked, picking him up by his middle.

"Ann Marie, may I suggest you and Tim take the Subaru to your house. I'll drive Katie home in your van after you've had a chance to get settled. And I won't mention anything to Katie about Bob. I'll leave that up to you two."

Standing, Ann placed Sassy back on the floor. "All right." She pushed the chair under the table before wrapping her arms around her father's middle and resting her head against his chest. "Thanks, Dad. I know telling me was hard."

She gave him a hug and said in a near whisper, "It's not fair. Why is it the good ones?"

Ann stepped outside into the bright sunshine and looked about, startled that life around her carried on as usual, without a mere sigh at Uncle Bob's passing. How could the world be the same without Uncle Bob in it?

It all seemed so strange and cast doubt over life's purpose.

But the birds continued to sing and flit from place to place, the lilacs continued to emit their luscious scent, and the sun's radiating warmth once again touched her skin.

How can any of this be?

■ ■ ■

Less than a week after burying Ann's uncle Bob in the Meyer family plot at Elmhurst Manor, not far from the bowling alley where Nell had invited Ann to tag along as a kid, devastating news struck once again with a heartless vengeance.

"Hey, Tim!" Ann hollered, bursting through the front door of the house, a heavy grocery sack in each arm. "The phone's ringing … Would you please get it? My hands are full."

"Sure! I'm coming!"

He emerged from the laundry room, dropping a basket of linens to the floor as he picked up the phone from its cradle on the kitchen counter.

"Yes, this is Tim Palmer. Yes, of course … I can be there in a few minutes, Sergeant Hoffman." He pushed the 'end' button with his thumbnail and returned the phone to its cradle as Ann slid the paper sacks past the counter's edge. "Huh, that's odd."

"What's odd? Where are you headed?"

"Down to the store … something's going on, but the sergeant wasn't specific … said he'd fill me in when I get there."

"Hmm, I was there thirty minutes ago … didn't seem to be

anything going on. I stopped by the bank after that." Ann threw her hands in the air and shrugged. "Maybe somebody got caught shoplifting."

"No ... the sergeant wouldn't call me down there for something that trivial."

"Do you want me to go with you, Tim?"

"No, that's okay," he replied, gathering his car keys. "I'll let you know what's going on the first chance I get."

"All right, don't forget, please."

He closed the front door behind him.

Aware of the fact that idle time attracted painful thoughts of Uncle Bob, Ann busied herself by putting the groceries away, facing all cans and packages in the same direction on the wide pantry shelves, and arranging the refrigerated foods by kind and frequency of use—items used most often placed in front.

Feeling energized, she started a load of laundry and folded the clean sheets and towels, their center creases in perfect alignment. Stepping back, Ann laughed at her handiwork.

Wow, bring out the straitjacket! Not the way Mother would've tackled things. I guarantee she'd be the first one to have me committed for being a neat freak!

I wonder how she's coping with Uncle Bob's death. It's strange ... the tension that seemed to exist between them. Nothing I can do, though. She'd never open up to me in a million years. Shrugging, Ann whipped up a marinade for the tri-tip steaks she'd purchased, adding an extra dash of Worcestershire sauce.

By the time she refrigerated the soaking meat, her thoughts had turned to Tim.

She looked at the stove clock. Forty minutes had passed.

"Darn him for not calling me by now. I might as well head to the store and find out what's going on for myself."

As Ann pulled up to the market moments later, the county's new ambulance slowly pulled away from the back of the building. *Oh, no, somebody must be ill.* She stepped out of the van and watched it turn onto the roadway. *Hmm ... why no lights and siren?* Ann felt a hand on her shoulder.

She whirled around and met her husband's doleful eyes, his complexion chalk white. "No, please don't tell me, Tim ... I can't take any more."

She buried her face in his chest.

"Dad's heart burst, Annie. The EMTs said it happened so fast that he wouldn't have felt anything ... thank God." He took her face in his broad hands and kissed her on the forehead. His voice broke. "Annie, he's with Mom now."

Chapter Fifteen

June 1988

Fred pumped the brakes on his consulting work, reducing his Denver commutes to three days once monthly. He then revved the engine and roared from one long-neglected house project to another—from power-washing decades of grime off the logs' exteriors to replacing the two fixed-glass family room windows with horizontal sliders to reviving the kitchen cabinets with new brushed nickel hardware and a fresh coat of yellow satin latex, the warm color of cornmeal.

As Fred's momentum gained hold, the notion of adding a sorely needed two-story addition increasingly occupied his thoughts. Discussions with Mabel rapidly progressed from the dining room table to the drawing board. Ann figured the idea of less face-to-face time with Mabel during and after construction fueled her father's relentlessness.

His days during the project would be spent overseeing the work, and after its completion, extra living space would mean more elbow room.

In no time, Fred had building plans in hand and a local contractor on-site.

After months of plastic partitions, seeping sawdust, and the weekly *buzz, clack, bam* orchestrated by the construction crew virtuosos, only a thorough clean-up and the staging of furniture and bric-a-brac remained. Rather than tossing a coin with Fred for dibs on the spacious new upstairs bedroom with its private deck overlooking Mt. Polk, Mabel—fighting a chronic cough—chose not to battle the stairs. Instead, she decided to stay put in Ann and Sarah's old bedroom downstairs—the single bedroom before the addition.

Mabel had said, "You can have the new upstairs bedroom, Fred. I'm sticking with the girls' old room. But I certainly intend to spend my days in the new living room on my chaise longue. It'll fit perfectly in front of the south-facing windows."

■ ■ ■

Tim backed Bubba up to Fred and Mabel's front door, jumped out, and lowered the tailgate. He put on his tatty leather gloves before tugging on the thick gray moving pad underneath the chaise longue, pulling it forward.

"Wait, Tim. I'd better check to see if Mother's home before we unload it," Ann said, traveling around to the back of the truck. "The Impala's gone, which is kinda strange. Dad knew we'd be here by ten o'clock, and he's always 'mister dependable.'"

"But it's not ten yet, right?"

"Close enough in my book." Ann checked her watch. "It's five minutes till." She rang the doorbell and gave the doorknob a twist. "Hmm, the door's locked." A mischievous grin brightened her face as she did a silly dance step and rang the bell again, winking at Tim. "Come on, Wicked Witch of the West!" Still, no one answered. She bent over and removed the house key from underneath the jute doormat.

Tim's forehead crinkled. "Not such a smart place to hide a key, wouldn't you say?"

"That's for sure. But wouldn't it be funny if someone let themselves in and stole Mother!" Ann crossed her fingers. "One can at least hope!" *Okay, that wasn't necessary.*

She pushed the door open, and Sassy and Rufus shot past her like two escaped convicts on the lam. "Mother, are you home? Hello?"

Ann sniffed the air.

"Mmm, smells like breakfast."

She slid the key back under the doormat and walked in, through the dining room, and into the kitchen. A full pan of bacon sat in solidified grease on a cold front burner.

Next to the stove, an egg carton and loaf of bread lay unopened on the counter. "Mother, where are you?" she asked, moving through the family room, past the couch where her father always slept, and into the bedroom.

The yellow daisy bedspread lay unevenly over the pillows, and her mother's faded black pajama set, now ash gray, hung off the side of the bed.

Ann bristled at the used tissues and splintered toothpicks littering the top of the bedside table. Lip curled, she walked over to the dresser. *Geez, what a mess. Looks like she turned her purse upside down and shook it.* She grimaced and shuddered, making her dangly earrings jiggle.

Retracing her steps through the family room, she noticed her father's bedding still sitting in a pile on the couch, which seemed odd.

The French doors leading into the new living room remained propped open—on one side by the antiquated canister vacuum Ann had used as a kid and on the other side by a cardboard box filled with cleaning supplies.

She snickered, knowing her father, not mother, planned on using them.

After slipping off her clogs, she tiptoed across the plush carpet, still bowled over by her parents' daring choice of eggplant purple.

"Hello! Mother, are you upstairs?"

She took the steps two at a time.

The room contained a few empty soda cans and a small pile of construction debris. "Okay, something's gotta be up with those two." Ann checked her wristwatch a second time as she stepped back through the front door. She shrugged and looked at Tim, puzzled. "Now it's after ten ... and I'm getting worried. Mother's left a full pan of cooked bacon on the stove and an unopened egg carton on the counter. It looks like they left in a hurry."

"No note, huh?"

"Not that I saw."

"Annie, I betcha a million bucks they got a late start and figured they'd better run a few errands before we arrived with the chair."

"Yeah ... maybe so. But ever since Uncle Bob and your dad passed away—"

"Honey, there's no sense worrying over something we know nothing about. Right?"

"Yeah, well—"

"Come on, Annie. First things first, let's get this chaise unloaded."

"Okay. You're right. I need to stop being such a worrywart, and remind me to tidy up the kitchen before we leave, please."

Ann removed her thin cotton gardening gloves from her back pocket and put them on. "You better walk backward so I don't slip out of my clogs."

The couple flipped the chair onto its side and proceeded, making slow progress as they wove it through the tight maze of walls and furniture. Once in the living room, Ann suggested they set it between the two south-facing windows.

"Mother also wants to put the Asian-looking armoire that's in the dining room in here. We might as well move it, too, huh?"

"Sure, no problem. Better check to see if it's empty, though."

Ann tugged on the two ornate brass knobs, pulling both doors open. "Yay, only a shoebox in here." She set the lidless box on the dining table and rifled through it. "Hmm ... a couple of folded documents and a bunch of pictures of Mother and Dad. Mind if I take a quick look at the photos?"

"No, have at it," Tim replied, taking off his gloves and tossing them beside the box.

He snuggled up behind Ann and kissed her on the back of the neck. "Hey, you little snoop!"

"Stop it, Romeo!" She slapped his broad shoulder in jest. "I wanna look through this stuff before they get back."

Ann held up a black-and-white photo.

"Look at this one! I forgot they used to bowl together on a league. I wish I had those funky bowling shirts ... they're worth money these days. There might be a date on the back." She turned the snapshot over and squinted at the numbers scrunched up in the bottom left-hand corner. "Um ... September 27, 1957."

"Well, that can't be right, Annie. You were born on October 21. That's less than a month later. Turn it over and look at your mom. She's as skinny as ever."

"Yeah, you're right. That's weird. She must have written the wrong year." Ann picked up the next picture. "Okay, Mother's fishing at the edge of a lake in pedal pushers and a form-fitting top ... definitely not pregnant, at least not noticeably."

Turning it over, she handed it to Tim to read.

"It was taken September 15, 1957, at Brommer Lake, wherever that is."

Ann dug into the middle of the thick stack, grabbing a handful of the black-and-white images, turning them upside down. "Look at these, will you? There has to be a mistake."

He read the dates: "October 2, 1957; September 23, 1957; August 30, 1957; October 20, 1957—"
"Give me that one." Ann gulped and seized it out of Tim's hand. "No way, she's standing sideways talking to someone in a friggin' tight shirtwaist dress. And Sarah thought she was the one who was adopted!" Ann shrieked, throwing the box on the floor. "What the hell?" She stomped out the front door, slamming it so hard that Mabel's favorite fruit still life fell off the adjacent wall.

Tim stayed behind to pick up the fallen print, checking to see that the glass hadn't cracked before rehanging it. He then knelt beside the box and repacked the photographs, verifying more dates at random. "April 10, 1961—the month and year Sarah was born." Although uncertain of the actual day, Tim knew her birthday fell at the end of the month. He turned the photo over to find Mabel as thin as a Triscuit and grinning like an overzealous politician, flanked arm in arm by two white-haired women in aprons. "Good Lord, Mabel!" he said, flicking her image with his fingertip. "What secrets are you hiding?"

Pushing himself up off the floor, Tim spotted a folded document, poking out from under a dining room chair. He bent over and picked it up, smoothing it open on the table. "Huh, a Colorado State Marriage License."

He recognized the tall, willowy strokes of Fred's signature but stopped at that of the bride's. "Ann Lynn Williams. Well, I'll be … you old devil, you were married before. Too bad for you that it didn't last. Funny, your bride's name was Ann." He glanced toward the ceiling, eyes narrowing. "That couldn't be why Mabel has such a grudge against Annie, right? Nah … that's ridiculous … it's a coincidence. Annie was named after both her grandmas, and Fred's mother's name was Ann."

Tim stepped to the center of the room and picked up the box.

Balancing it against his hip with one arm, he fished for the second document.

"Gotcha!"

He returned the box to the bottom shelf of the armoire before unfolding the document. "Of course, it figures that it's another marriage license. This time from Texas ... Mabel June Meyer and Lawrence William Radnor."

Tim refolded both documents and slipped them under the photos at the bottom of the box. "More than a few *skeletons* in this closet, that's for sure." He pushed the armoire doors closed and grabbed his gloves off the table on his way out of the house.

Ann sat on the passenger side of Bubba, staring straight ahead, her stocking feet on the dashboard. Tim closed the tailgate and climbed in, contemplating how she might take this new information.

Relief rippled across his face as Ann donned an unexpected grin.

"The more I think about it, maybe this isn't so all-fired bad after all. If it turns out that I'm adopted, it means that I'm not genetically related to *her*. Yes!" she said, raising a fist in victory. "That'd be better than winning the lottery!"

Speechless, Tim stopped staring at Ann, released the emergency brake, and turned the key in the ignition. Bubba groaned to life and slowly weaved across the washboard driveway like a Weeble in a parade. Fighting against the lack of power steering, he made a wide right-hand turn onto Steele Street.

"Do you think your parents would admit to it even if it were true?"

"Hardly! Look who you're talking about! Mr. Don't-Upset-Your-Mother and Mrs. I-Don't-Want-to-Hear-about-It. Their motto must be 'Pretend certain things don't exist, and they don't.' Those two are the most tight-lipped people on this earth."

Ann balled up her fists and scrunched her reddening face, growling.

"Ewwww, they make me mad!"

Tim glanced at his wife.

"Now, Annie, this is merely a suggestion, but how about writing a letter to each county courthouse in Colorado to see if they have adoption records on you? If you were adopted, chances are it took place in the same state. That way, by searching the records yourself, any denials from Fred and Mabel can be rebutted—if you want to."

He flipped on the left blinker and gave the wheel a hard yank into their driveway.

Ann cocked her head to one side and, with brows knotted, studied Tim's suggestion. "You're right; I'll do it! As soon as we're finished with lunch, I'll write a rough draft."

Even before the truck came to a complete stop, she pushed the door open. With the lined curtains still closed, the inside of the house felt ten degrees cooler than the mild seventy-two degrees outside.

Ann tugged on the drapery cords, watching the light swoop through the living room like angels to her rescue, while Tim checked the answering machine on the kitchen counter, its tiny red light blinking its silent code.

After the first sharp beep, Mabel's voice droned on. "Oh, how I hate talking to these dumb machines! Ann Marie, where are you? This is your mother. Your father's had a mild heart attack … and we're here at St. Joseph's Hospital in Colorado Springs. Call me."

"Oh, no!" Ann cupped both hands over her mouth, eyes pleading. "If anything happens to him—"

"Hold on, Annie, she said 'mild.' Let's calm down and look at the caller ID so I can write down the phone number."

He picked up the handset and reached inside the wicker basket next to the phone cradle for a pen and paper.

Ann slipped off her clogs and sprinted up the stairs. She slid open the mirrored closet door, stood on her tiptoes, and pulled down a pair of folded jeans from the top shelf, draping them over one arm. With her free hand, she struggled to remove two short-sleeve tops from their plastic hangers. Tossing the clothing on the bed, she also gathered enough socks and underwear for several days.

"Hey, sweetie," Tim said as he came into the bedroom, "I tried the number several times but didn't get an answer."

"Maybe we'd better head to the hospital, Tim," she replied, snatching her canvas duffle bag from under the bed. "What do you think?"

"Okay, but you do realize I'm gonna have to come back home tonight, so I can work tomorrow, don't you?"

"Ugh! I know, and it means that I'm going to have to ride home with Mother if I stay. What a stinking, lousy time for the van to be in the shop for repairs! And I know poor old Bubba wouldn't make the trip."

"All right, I'll call Katie at her friend's house and tell her we'll pick her up in fifteen minutes. How much longer are you going to be?"

"Give me five minutes. I need to grab a few toiletries and toss them in the bag. I'll meet you at the car." Ann wrapped her arms around his soft pudgy waist and leaned her full weight into him.

She took a deep breath. "I hope he's going to be okay."

"Me, too." Tim gave her a tight squeeze. "I shouldn't have insisted on staying to unload the chair. I'm sorry."

"Well, if we'd have come straight home, we wouldn't have found those photos." Ann pulled back from his embrace and took hold of his hands. "If those pictures mean what they seem to … they'll be life-changing."

■ ■ ■

With Fred dozing in his hospital bed after a successful balloon angioplasty procedure and Tim and Katie on their way home, Mabel decided that she and Ann could celebrate with dinner and a movie. Mother and daughter checked *The Gazette* in the hospital lobby, settling on the 7:25 p.m. showing of *Rain Man* at the Citadel Mall. Upon Mabel's prodding, Ann led the way through the throngs of people swarming around the fast-food restaurants in the mall's food court, imagining her mother's eyes fixed in disgust on the deformed hump of flesh and bone between her shoulder blades. She took a step, dropped her narrow shoulders, and pushed them together like a far-out dance move, wishing Sarah had taken a few days off from her graduate studies to act as a buffer, as she did during their childhood.

Ann stepped out of the main flow of traffic and stopped.

"Does anything look good to you, Mother?"

"I'm going to get a fish sandwich and fries at McDonald's. And maybe a milkshake."

"Okay. I'll have the same."

Mabel gestured once again for Ann to lead the way.

The line moved quickly. Ann placed her order first and paid, putting the change in her wallet.

Oh, no! Is this all the money I have left? She stepped to one side and fumbled through her purse for extra cash and her checkbook but came up empty-handed.

"I believe I'll have a small vanilla milkshake," Mabel said to the clerk.

Taking slow, even breaths, Ann attempted to relax and shifted her focus to her mother. "Is that all you're getting? You said you wanted a fish sandwich."

"The milkshake will do." Mabel dropped the change into her zippered coin purse.

The two women spotted a vacant dining table and sat down. Ann opened two ketchup packets and poured them over her fries. She held the paper pouch out toward Mabel. "Would you like some fries?"

Mabel shook her head and took a long sip of her shake.

"Dad looks good. What a relief that he won't need open-heart surgery." Ann took a bite of her sandwich, swiping the corners of her mouth with her thin paper napkin. "How long does the doctor plan on keeping him in the hospital?"

Slow to respond, Mabel unzipped her bag and rummaged for a tissue before looking into Ann's tired face and giving her shoulders a shrug.

Although stymied by the reason behind her mother's *silent game,* Ann felt anger percolate through her veins.

She leaned both elbows on the tabletop and uncrossed her feet, planting them squarely on the tiled floor to keep from bolting to the nearest payphone and begging for rescue by an old schoolmate who lived close to the mall.

Her mind returned to the photos she and Tim had found this morning.

After returning home, she planned to prove her adoption theory. *'The fur will fly' then, as your old expression goes, Mother.*

Ann forced herself to take slow, deep breaths and transported herself and her fast-food meal to a warm, sunny beach while Mabel sat in silence, scanning through brochures on heart health.

"I'm finally finished, Mother. Are you ready to head over to the cinema? We're early, but I bet they'll have lots of previews to watch."

Mabel stood up. "No, thank you. I've changed my mind. I want to go back to the Super 8."

"Gosh, are you sure?" *I'd much rather look at Tom Cruise's face for the next two hours than be held prisoner behind a locked motel room door with you as my cellmate, even if we do have separate beds!*

Suddenly, Ann's cheeks glowed scarlet as she remembered she didn't have enough money to go anyway.

"Yes, I'm sure." Giving Ann her back, Mabel led the way out through the food court to the main mall entrance. Once outside, she spun around and leaned in close to her eldest child, her breath thick like buttermilk. "Ann Marie, you'll never change ... you selfish ... little twit! Do you have any idea how much you humiliated me in there?"

Ann froze and stared at her mother's misshapen mouth, the words biting into her flesh. She felt as rattled as she had this morning after discovering the photos of her model-slim mother. Barely audible, she said, "What?"

"You heard me! You humiliated me when you didn't offer to pay for my dinner in front of that McDonald's girl!" Mabel shook her finger in Ann's face. "You're such an embarrassment to me! You've been an embarrassment to me your whole life, Turtle!"

Mabel covered her mouth, fighting hard to stifle a cough.

Tears welled up in Ann's eyes, and the elderly couple who stopped to stare went unnoticed. "I didn't mean to embarrass you," she replied, voice squeaky. "We left the house in such a hurry after we listened to your message that I forgot to grab extra cash. I arrived with eight dollars in my wallet. If I'd have known you weren't getting anything more than a shake, I'd have paid."

Ann wiped away her tears.

"I don't understand you, Mother. All I want is for us to be friendly to each other like most mothers and daughters. You seem to hate me no matter what I do."

Mabel turned away.

The two women walked in single file to the Impala. Ann pressed her body against the passenger door and fixed her gaze beyond the city lights, which flashed like mortar fire as Mabel torpedoed past them, block after block.

Back at the motel, sleep took Mabel early, her loud and throaty snores causing Ann to lose sleep. *Ewwww, I wish I had the guts to smother you with this friggin' pillow, you ... eternal child!* At last, she stripped the thin blanket and bedspread off her bed, clutched her two pillows by the edge of their cases, and retreated to the bathtub, where she made herself a porcelain nest of sorts. Within moments, discomfort succumbed to sheer exhaustion. As she fell motionless, the Sandman whisked her away to the same tropical beach of her dinnertime escape from Mabel.

Chapter Sixteen

September 1992

The last drops of water trickled from the pitcher into the misshapen bowl. "Sorry to disappoint you, fellas, but it's only water," Ann said as her two rowdy puppies, Bernie and Gus, sniffed the metal basin. She placed the pitcher in the kitchen sink before scooping up the crinkled geranium plant leaves on the windowsill in front of her. As she tossed the debris into the trashcan underneath the sink, Gus flopped down across her tennis shoes, nibbling the newly replaced shoestrings.

"No, you don't, mister … not again!"

Ann lowered herself to the floor and coaxed the puppies onto her lap.

A barrage of wet kisses gave her the giggles. "Man, you two rascals are growing fast. Heaven help us when you fit into your basset-sized paws!"

She removed several small dog treats from her jeans pocket, skimming them across the terracotta tiles and out into the living room. Using the counter's edge, she pulled herself up and brushed the fawn-colored dog hair from her clothes.

With the geranium clean-up crossed off her lengthy to-do list, Ann resolved to knock out one more chore before lunch.

She plopped down on the dark leather sofa and skimmed through a half-dozen tasks for something that would trigger the least amount of reluctance: 1) clean fish tank, 2) ready VHS tapes for yard sale, 3) box up clothes not worn within last twelve months, 4) clean underneath fridge, 5) prune terrarium plants, or 6) dust mini blinds. *Screw the blinds and the fish tank. Closet ... nope ... that's an all-day job.*

She removed a stubby pencil from a squat wide-mouthed vase on the coffee table—Katie's pottery project from Girl Scout Camp the summer after sixth grade—and drew a line through chore number five.

Anything to stop dwelling on this adoption mess for a while.

Four years had passed since she and Tim had found the questionable photos of Mabel.

A *miserable* four years.

If it wasn't an argument with Tim regarding her refusal to confront her parents, it was her constant plotting to avoid them. Through it all, her tried-and-true excuse remained the same: a confrontation on the subject with her parents would send her father into cardiac arrest.

Ann stood up. "All right, boys, those plants aren't going to prune themselves, are they?" She shooed the puppies from underneath her feet and proceeded to the kitchen, tossing the list on the counter. Fishing through the junk drawer, she snagged the pair of stainless steel embroidery scissors once used on Katie's nails.

"Ahhh! She was so little then."

Where in the world have the last fourteen years gone?

Deciding that the pruning might be less messy on the kitchen counter, Ann walked over to the oak buffet in the dining room, jockeyed her hands underneath the large glass container, and lifted.

"Oh, my!" *I forgot how heavy this is. Forget it! This jar's not going anywhere.* She removed the round lid, setting it upside down to prevent condensation from damaging the top of the buffet. Untying the night-blue bandana from around her neck, Ann spread it out next to the terrarium as a catch for the trimmings.

With a surgeon's precision, she snipped and pinched. Miniature ceramic figurines, before hidden by the overgrowth, abruptly emerged: a lioness and her two cubs; a pair of geese in a high-gloss finish; an African elephant, its trunk raised above its head; three grazing zebras; a momma skunk and her kit; and a turtle encrusted in hardened soil. Ann removed the whole lot—a fraction of the collection Grammy and Grandpa Fred had started for Katie after returning from an African safari—and carried them to the kitchen sink.

She dampened the corner of the plaid dishrag, added a small dab of dish detergent, and gently scrubbed the turtle's olive-green shell.

"Ouch, Gus!" she said, startled as he ran full-throttle into the back of her leg.

A tiny *ping* sounded in the damp porcelain sink.

Ann grimaced and dared to look inside.

"Uh-oh, it's the turtle's head!"

She pinched the head between her thumb and index finger and held it up to the window, close to her bespectacled face. "At least it's a clean break. A drop of Super Glue and the turtle will be as good as new." She set both pieces inside a teacup perched on the windowsill among the geraniums to let them dry. Then, to prevent another such mishap, she coaxed the puppies inside the utility room with rawhide treats and closed the door.

Soon the clean herd of miniatures dried in the dish drainer while Ann aerated the terrarium's chocolate-brown soil with a dinner fork, breathing in its fresh, earthy scent. *Mmm, that takes me back to Uncle Bob's ranch.*

Eyes closed, Ann drifted on the childhood memory of combing through newly plowed fields for arrowheads with her uncle Bob.

■ ■ ■

Tim slid his hand along the stair rail as he inched his way down the carpeted steps in the murky dark of early morning. "There you are," he said, looking at Ann's silhouette against the nightlight's dim glow. Faint curlicues of citrus-scented steam rose from the mug of tea she held up to her mouth. He flipped on the overhead fixture.

"Thinking about those blasted photos again?"

"No, for once, I'm not."

"Why are you up so early then?"

"Well, believe me, it's not by choice." Ann squinted from the intrusion of light. "I woke up from this bizarre dream and couldn't fall back to sleep." She held up Katie's algebra textbook. "I even tried reading through those horrid story problems you helped Katie solve last night." A half-smile tugged at her lips. "That kinda stuff switched my brain to snooze mode in high school."

Tim filled the coffee carafe with tap water. "Well, that's not how I remember it. You used to throw those newspaper measurement terms around like crazy—pica, column inch, and ... help me, Annie."

"Point?"

"Yes, that's it. And all that measuring called for tricky formulas. Next time Katie needs help, you're elected."

"Oh, brother! Tell me, how in the world can you be so chipper in the morning? You must be doing drugs."

"Ha! Nope ... high on life," Tim replied with a smirk, dropping two pieces of wheat bread into the toaster. "Okay, so what about your dream? The short version, though," he added, glancing at the stove clock. "I need to be at the store for a delivery in thirty minutes."

Ann took a sip of tea. "Umm ... It's rather embarrassing."

"Go on. That's never stopped you before."

"Okay. Well, I was something of a ... *creature feature*, you might say ... in a cartoonish-looking booth at this outdoor carnival. My head was my own, but my arms and legs were those of a giant turtle. And on my back was this pitched stone-like shell plastered with dried-on bits of food."

Tim snorted so hard that he dropped his jellied toast down the front of his T-shirt. "Darn!"

Ann donned a shocked smile. "Shh! You're going to wake Katie, not to mention our two furballs in the laundry room!"

He scraped off a glob of jelly with his fingertip and stuck it in his mouth.

"Mmm ... good."

Ann covered her mouth to stifle a laugh.

Lowering his voice to a whisper, Tim wiped the smirk off his face with his fingertips and said, "Okay, go on." He took a bite of toast and leaned forward.

"As best as I can figure, the object of the game was to hit my head with food from this gooey smorgasbord while I quickly wobbled back and forth to this funky tune called 'The Broken Turtle Blues.'"

She snorted twice. "Uh-oh! Now I'm the noisemaker!"

"Tell me, Annie, should I eat this other piece of toast or fling it at you?"

She held up her index finger. "Hold on ... not much longer." Inhaling deeply, she continued, "Each time a contestant hit my head with a spoonful of food, it exploded into pieces like a piñata, spilling out trinkets—skeleton rings, rubber balls that looked like bloodshot eyes, freakish figurines, along with other weird stuff— that they'd pick from. The game was then put on hold while I grew a new head in front of the crowd."

Tim pointed to the clock.

"Okay, one more minute ... I promise!" She sped up the narration.

"The last contestants were none other than my parents. I remember watching in terror as Mother dipped this humongous serving spoon into the mashed potatoes and took aim while Dad cheered her on."

"Then what?"

Ann shrugged, flinging her hands in the air. "I woke up!"

Tim frowned and folded his arms across his chest. "What brought on such a weird dream? Been watching too many *Twilight Zone* reruns?"

Ann slid off the stool and shuffled over to the windowsill in her fluffy slippers. "Here's the culprit." She removed the broken figurine's head and body from the teacup and held them in her palm.

"I broke the turtle a few days ago when I was cleaning out the terrarium and put the pieces in the teacup for safe keeping till I could glue them back together. But now, I think I'll throw them away."

She folded her fingers over her palm, shook the two pieces together like a pair of dice, and cast them against the backsplash.

There, they shattered into smaller parts. "Snake eyes," she said, mumbling to herself.

At that moment, Ann's breath caught in her throat, and her head felt as light as a bubble. She looked at the jagged bits and pieces, her mother immediately coming to mind. *Whoa...crazy! I can't believe it's taken this long to figure things out ... but hey, I don't have to live like this. No more shy-turtle, humped-back crap!*

It's over! Like it or not, Mommy dearest, I can't change how I look, but I can change the way I look at myself. And how I see you and Dad, too.

Tim grabbed Ann's shoulder.

"You all right? You looked like you zoned out for a minute."

Ann turned with a start. "What, huh ... oh, yes. I'm fine."

Better than you can imagine.

"Good." Tim placed his coffee mug in the sink. "And as for your dream, you'll have to figure it out on your own. But instead of being ... um ... a 'creature feature,' I prefer to think of you as being ... *a-dork-able!*" He caressed Ann's shoulder, his broad smile beneath raised eyebrows. "Get it?"

Ann mustered a feeble laugh before turning back to the sink.

"Okay, that probably wasn't my best attempt at humor. Or maybe it's too early in the morning, huh?" He kissed the top of her head. "Anyway, I need to shower. I don't want to be late to the store."

Moments later, as Tim turned on the water upstairs, the pipes sounded an eerie rendition of "Reveille." Bernie and Gus joined in from the laundry room, going from sporadic yowls to full-out howls in record time.

"Okay, boys, move back." Ann pushed the door open a smidgen and slid through. The newspaper that had covered the floor the night before lay strewn about in a confetti maze.

Ann navigated through the clutter to the back door, wading against the tide of prancing paws. She opened the door wide. "Charge!"

The duo rushed outside, crisscrossing back and forth, their noses to the ground.

■ ■ ■

By the time Katie paraded into the kitchen—her freshly scrubbed face contradicting her sleepy droop—Ann had a plan in mind.

First, however, she'd have to get Katie off to school. Then she'd get down to business.

Explanations would come soon enough.

"Good morning, Katydid," she said, giving her daughter an animated once-over.

"Where in the world did you get that cool top and jean jacket?"

Katie shook her head. "Oh, brother, Mom! We both know you bought them for me." She opened the cupboard door next to the refrigerator and pulled out a granola bar.

"Want a glass of milk to go with that?"

"No, don't we have any more juice pouches? I'd rather take one of those with me and drink it at school. I'm not hungry right now."

"Check the cupboard again. There should be a few on the shelf above the granola bars."

"Yep, there are." Katie slipped a pouch into the side pocket of her backpack. "Have you seen my algebra book?"

Ann lifted it up off the stool beside her and held it out, the edges of Katie's folded homework assignment poking out from between the pages. "Here you go."

"Thanks, Mom." Katie stuffed the textbook inside the top of her pack and made a straight line for the front door, stopping long enough to pat Bernie and Gus.

"Hey, what does a mom have to do to get a kiss around here these days?"

Katie touched her fingertips to her lips and blew her mother a kiss.

Before Ann could reciprocate, the front door slammed shut. "I love you, too!" She smirked. "Aren't teenagers grand?"

As Ann heard the school bus' motor rev and pull away from the driveway, she hopped off the stool and hurried into the living room, over to the top drawer of the drop-leaf desk.

She searched through an assortment of stationery, selecting two sheets of pastel green parchment with a narrow band of white diamonds linked together across the top like a string of paper dolls. "Nice!" She addressed a matching envelope and set it aside. With a loud exhale, Ann lowered the tip of the black ink pen to the paper, concentrating on using her best hand.

9/17/92

Dear Aunt Nell,

I hope this note finds you well.

I can't count the number of times I've picked up the phone in the last four years to call you with a particular question. But now, I've decided this question might be best received in a letter.

As you know, Sarah's believed since early childhood that she was adopted. And until 1988, after running across photos of Mother in which—according to the dates—she should've been noticeably pregnant with me but wasn't, I'd thought her suspicions were ridiculous.

Then Tim found several photos of Mother dated days before Sarah's birth, and again, she was as thin in those pictures as she is today.

As bold as this question must be, Aunt Nell, are we both adopted?

I'm sorry to throw this in your lap. I can't tell you how much I've agonized over whether to ask you or not, yet I know it's the best way to find out. Mother will never tell me, will never be honest with me the way you will.

I also don't know how else to obtain an honest, speedy answer. Tim suggested I write to each county courthouse in the state. However, after giving it much consideration, the task seems too daunting. It's not only that, though; I also know you'll be on my side—helping me—as usual. And I love you for it—for being yourself.

Thank you for your honesty. It means the world to me that I can trust your answer, with no doubts whatsoever.

*All my love,
Annie*

P.S. I haven't told Sarah yet about the photos and will wait until I hear from you.

After rereading each paragraph word by word, Ann folded the stationery into thirds and slipped it into the readied envelope, hoping it didn't sound too formal.

Finally, she blessed the sealed letter with the solemnity of the Pope and carried it to their mailbox at the end of the driveway.

Pulling open its rounded door, she tossed the envelope inside for fear she'd change her mind. With a swift flip of her wrist, she raised the red metal flag on its side into its upright position. "Bon voyage!" she said, slamming its door shut, her heart skipping a beat. Ann gazed at the dark, angry thunderheads gathering to the southeast.

A loud drum roll from the heavens would've been a fitting omen!

Chapter Seventeen

October 1992

Ann lay across the top of the hand-quilted comforter, her stocking feet dangling off the side of the double bed. She clutched the cordless phone tight to her chest, agitated from her conversation with Aunt Nell.

"Ouch! Knock it off, you two! You're not coming up here!" she said to Bernie and Gus, who yipped and pawed at the soles of her feet. "Scramoose!"

Tossing the phone toward the head of the bed, she shook her feet free and rolled onto her side, hugging her legs to her middle.

What were the odds we hadn't been adopted? A zillion to one?

So many things make sense now. But why all the secrecy?

Aunt Nell said the social worker was adamant that kids should know they're adopted from the start ... be taught songs or rhymes about being a 'chosen' child.

Ann hit the mattress with her fist and let out a phlegm-retching *yech!*

"*Chosen* child, my ass! I'd give anything to have been *chosen* by a mother who thought of me as worth loving ... a mother who didn't see me as one stinking humiliation after another."

She squeezed her eyes shut.

It's as though the two of 'em stopped by some friggin' meat market and said, "Yes, Sir, we'll take the skinny, sullen one in the back row of case number one—the one who might otherwise not get 'chosen.' She has dark hair and eyes like we do. It'll be easy to fool her."

But what were you thinking with Sarah ... bright green eyes, red hair?

I bet you both about died the first time she asked you if she was adopted.

Ann opened her eyes with a start. *How am I going to tell Sarah?* The phone rang. "Oh, no, I can't talk to anyone right now! The last thing I want to do is be cordial!" *Damn it!*

She retrieved the phone from where it had landed behind the pillow and checked the caller ID with a groan. *Speak of the devil!* Ann cleared her throat, drew in a deep breath, and picked up on the final ring. "Hey, Sarah."

"Well, hello there. I'm glad you answered. I was ready to hang up. How's it going? I haven't talked to you in a while."

"Well, funny you should ask," Ann replied, voice thin and wavering. "Aren't you due for a trip this direction?"

"Why? Is something going on? You sound off-kilter."

"Can't a sister want a little sister time?"

"Yeah, Annie, but it's a long drive for a little *sister time.* Plus the fact, the weather can be pretty crummy mid-October, as you well know. We might as well wait until Thanksgiving. Don't you think?"

"I don't know if I can wait another six weeks." *Shoot, I shouldn't have said that!* Ann tapped her forehead in disbelief.

"All right, now I'm worried. Is something wrong with Mom or Daddy?"

"No, they're both doing—"

"What about Katie and Tim?" Sarah interrupted, the words leaping from her tongue.

"No. Trust me. I need to talk with you in person."

"Good heavens, Annie, why? Are *you* sick? Did something happen to you?"

Ann took a deep breath before speaking. "This isn't how I wanted to tell you, Sarah."

"Tell me what? Spit it out!"

"Okay, don't blow a gasket!" She shook her head, eyes squeezed shut. "Oh, Sarah, you've been right all along about being adopted. But it wasn't only you. Both of us were adopted as babies from an orphanage called the Colorado State Children's ... something or other ... in Denver."

"Who says?"

"Aunt Nell. I got off the phone with her a few minutes ago. She told me that she and Uncle Bob had disagreed from the get-go with Mother and Dad's decision to keep our adoption a secret from us. And they vowed they'd tell us the truth if we ever asked them."

"Well, I'll be damned! But don't scare me like that again, Annie. I had all kinds of horrible stuff running through my head—you have cancer, you'd been raped, you—"

"Okay, geez!" Ann withered down into the bedspread. "Give me a break. Please."

Sarah's words materialized at a sluggish pace.

"I'm sorry, Annie ... I truly am. What a shock to hear the truth. Not that I'm surprised by it. The fact that they lied to me, to us, pisses me off!"

She groaned. "Remember Mom talking way back when about a great-uncle Clancy who I was supposed to resemble? What a crock!"

She lowered her voice. "But most of all, I feel an overwhelming sense of relief that I'm not biologically related to her ... that crazy, miserable woman."

Ann put on a puckish grin.

"Me, too. I had the same reaction!"

Scooting up toward the head of the bed, she took a sip of lukewarm water from last night's glass on her bedside table.

"You know, I've always felt a level of friction between Aunt Nell and Mother ... but wow, did Aunt Nell give it a voice today ... even referred to her as a barracuda!"

"Yep! Voracious and opportunistic ... that she is! But tell me, Annie, after all these years, what made you ask her now—at age 34?"

"Are you sitting down?"

"Yeah. But *please*, the *short version*!"

Her sister's choice of words made Ann smile. *Poor Sarah's heard her fair share of my 'long stories.' This one's a doozy, though ... deserves more than a few words!*

"All right, here goes." Ann propped her pillows against the headboard and leaned back. "It all started the morning Dad had his heart attack. Tim and I were alone at their house delivering a chaise longue Mother had ordered from a store in Silvermile. Of course, we didn't know at the time that anything had happened to Dad. We figured they were out running errands."

"What does this have to do with the adoption?"

"I'm getting to it." Ann took another sip of water. "After we unloaded the chair and moved it into the new addition, we figured we might as well move Mother's Asian armoire in there, too, as she wanted. And when I emptied it, I found a small box of snapshots of her and Dad. A number of them showed a skinny Mother when she should've been enormously pregnant with me, according to the dates written on the back. Tim later pulled out a few photos of her dated right before your birth. And again, wafer-thin! Obviously, something was out of whack."

"I don't understand why you waited till today to call Aunt Nell. Daddy's heart attack was years ago. And how about me? Why didn't you tell me right away?"

"I wanted proof before I told you, Sarah. And as far as Aunt Nell goes, I kept putting it off ... call me a coward." *I certainly have!* "It wasn't until last week that I sent her a letter. I figured it'd be too awkward to suddenly call her up and drop the question in her lap. Then she called me today."

"Hmm ... good thinking, Annie."

Ann scooted toward the middle of the bed and sat cross-legged.

"I also put off asking Aunt Nell because I didn't want to stir up the waters and rock the proverbial boat. It's like the old saying goes, 'Ignorance is bliss.'"

"Boy, that's the Castle mentality, all right. We've learned well, haven't we?"

"Yes, we have. Except, this time around, the ignorance wasn't so blissful."

Ann groaned. "I also worried that a confrontation with us might cause Dad to have another heart attack. But I'm up for a little rockin' and rollin' now. How about you? I don't want to confront them alone."

"Heavens, no! This is something we need to do together. Let me check with my supervisor tomorrow. I promise, one way or another, I'll be home in a few days."

"Thanks, Sarah. I should be able to avoid them until you arrive."

"Yeah, I had my regular weekly chat with Daddy yesterday, so I'll be off the hook as well." Sarah's voice softened. "We'll get through this, Annie. We deserve to know the truth ... we're worthy of it ... both of us. It's a basic child's right to know where she came from. And we deserve to try to obtain our biological family's medical history if we choose to."

"I agree," Ann said, on the verge of tears. "And you deserved to know about the pictures right after we found them. I can be such a chicken. I'm sorry, Sarah. Please, know that I love you."

"Hey, you obviously weren't ready to deal with this mess at the time, Annie. I promise I'll call you tomorrow after I confirm things with my boss. And I love you, too. Be sure to get some rest."

"I will. Thanks for understanding. I'll see you in a few days. Bye."

Ann set the phone on Tim's bedside table and walked over to the mirrored closet doors, stepping close and removing her glasses. With a sculptor's fingertips, she watched her reflection as she slowly traced back and forth across her face, her features appearing fragile. As she lowered her hand, she gazed at her palm, transfixed by the creases crisscrossing the surface, wishing she could decipher her distant past as well as her future.

This is bizarre. I feel like I've been thrown out of a moving car.
She dropped both hands to her sides.

The doe-eyes staring back in the mirror begged for answers.
Who am I? Do I look like somebody out there in the world? Does that somebody wonder about me?

■ ■ ■

Katie leaned back in the dining room chair, her black sneakers hooked around its front legs. She drummed her fingers against the tabletop, keeping time with the kitchen radio.

"Well ... it's weird, Mom, but ... kinda cool at the same time! I guess it means we have another family out there somewhere. You're not going to tell me that I'm adopted, too, are you?"

"Fat chance, Katydid. Don't you remember those glorious stretch marks etched across my belly?"

"Yes!" Katie covered her eyes. "Please don't show me those things again!"

"Ewwww! Yeah, please don't!" Sarah added, cackling. "I don't want to lose my appetite any more than I already have."

Ann shook her finger. "Haha, you two clowns!"

"Okay, I'll be serious now. Do Grammy and Grandpa Fred know you guys are going over to talk to 'em about being adopted?"

Sarah nodded. "Yeah, I called them when I arrived this afternoon."

Katie glanced from her aunt to her mother. "Are you nervous?"

"Nope, there's nothing to be nervous about. If things get out of hand, I'll pull out my pistol, right, Annie?"

Katie gasped and clutched her throat. "Really, Aunt Sarah?"

"Good grief, no, Katie. She's joking." Ann looked goggle-eyed at her sister. "That's not funny!"

Katie wrapped her hands around the sides of her face. "Yes, it is, Mom!"

"Okay, enough is enough! Sarah, I vote we head over now and get this over with."

"Fine by me. Let's go."

Katie pretended to pout. "I wish I could sneak along."

"No need. I promise your mom and I will fill you in when we get back."

Katie's shoulders fell. "Well, please don't be too hard on 'em. I can't help but feel kinda sorry for 'em. Remember, they're getting old."

"I know. It's a tough situation for everybody," Ann replied, gathering her purse and keys. "Oh, honey, will you please let the dogs in from out back? I forgot."

"Sure, Mom."

Sarah blew Katie a kiss and closed the front door.

■ ■ ■

The late afternoon sun bid an early adiós as a thick layer of dark clouds lumbered in from the south. Sarah covered her eyes and squinted at Mt. Polk.

"Yikes, looks like it could snow. The weatherman was right for a change." She hopped into the van and buckled her seat belt. "I might be staying with you for a few extra days."

"Of course," Ann replied, turning right onto Steele Street. She slid her glasses down to the tip of her nose, planted her eyes on her sister, and said in her best hillbilly voice, "Unless it goes sa good wid Ma and Pa Kettle dat ya wanna stay wid 'em for a spell!"

In turn, Sarah pointed to the cattle grazing on the other side of the roadway and shot back with a thumbs-down and her own hillbilly drawl. "Ya, when dem thar cows done fly ta da moon 'n back!"

The duo grinned like goons.

Ann parked the van behind their father's car and dropped the keys inside her purse. Both women unbuckled their seatbelts, but neither moved toward the door handles.

Ann held her hands out in front of her. "Geez, look at how shaky I am."

"Take a deep breath. At least it's an even playing field—two to two. Now, any sage advice from my big sister?"

"Me? You're the one they like!"

"Damn it, Annie, listen to the two of us as nervous as cats. What's with that?"

"Don't you see? It's like we said the other day over the phone. We've learned our lessons well at the hands of an all-time master of levity."

"Daddy, you mean?"

"Of course, Sarah! How do you think I survived the last thirty-some years of Mother and Dad's crap? Sprinkle glitter on the difficult or unpleasant things in life. Add rhinestones. Smile. Be friggin' congenial!" She looked at her lap, fidgeting with her purse straps.

"Mother's mentally ill," Ann continued, "and Dad's her chief enabler. We've tossed that idea around before. Aunt Nell told me that Uncle Bob tried to get Mother to see a mental health counselor for years, but she always put her foot down. Not surprisingly, she'd turn on him in a rant and then ignore the two of them for months on end. At least now the long lapses between our visits to their ranch make more sense."

Nodding, Sarah said, "This is off the subject of Mom being a nutcase, but other people besides Uncle Bob and Aunt Nell would've known we'd been adopted, right?"

"Practically everybody knew but us!" Ann took hold of Sarah's forearm. "Aunt Nell told me that was the main reason Mother and Dad pulled up stakes and moved us to Clifton. They were afraid someone was going to let the truth slip out within earshot of us. And that's why we didn't do much with our relatives who had kids … why we didn't have a chance to get to know our cousins."

"How could Mom and Daddy stoop so low as to ask our relatives to protect *their* secret? All to keep us from the truth. Oh, that pisses me off!"

Ann caught movement at the front door and released Sarah's arm.

"Great. It looks like Dad's motioning us inside. You ready?"

"As ready as I can be," Sarah replied, reaching for the door handle.

Fred—drowning in a baggy sweatsuit—stepped back, holding the front door open.

"Hello, girls," he said, lips stretched tight. "Come in."

Sarah entered first and removed her jacket, draping it across the back of a dining room chair. "Here, Annie, let me take your coat."

"Sure." Ann slipped her arms free and handed it to Sarah. "Thanks." Hands shaking, she turned up the cuffs of her blouse.

Speaking in a voice so faint that both daughters had to practically read his lips, Fred said, "Your mom's lying on the couch in the family room. She's not feeling well."

Ann nodded and led the way.

Of course, she's 'not well.' The jig's up!

Mabel pulled both hands out from underneath the afghan, pointed to the adjacent sofa, and said through a weak smile, "Have a seat, Sarah and Ann Marie."

Arms trembling, she reached for Fred's hand. "Here, help me sit up, will you?"

Wow, you've got the theatrics down pat, Mother!

Once their parents settled side by side, Sarah leaned forward, forearms planted on her thighs. "First of all, I hope we can get through this like four mature adults ... calmly and truthfully." She cranked her head around to look at her sister. "And if you don't mind, Annie, I'd like to start."

"By all means, go ahead."

"Mom, Daddy, first, why didn't you tell me the truth when I asked you if I was adopted? It would've been the perfect opportunity to tell us both. I can't even count the number of times I asked you when I was growing up."

Mabel sat up straighter. "The people at the orphanage advised us not to tell you. That's the way it was done back then."

Ann winced at the antiquated term *orphanage*.

She found herself making a fist and grinding her knuckles into her kneecap. She swallowed hard. "Maybe at other places, but not the Colorado State Children's Home. After the mid-1950s, the social workers there encouraged adoptive parents to be upfront and honest with their kids."

"How would you know?" Mabel asked with the same scowl Ann had seen many times. "Who told you that?"

Before Ann could answer, Mabel stood up, wagging her bony finger within inches of her oldest daughter's nose.

"You act like you're so high and mighty ... you and your gabby aunt! That's who told you, huh? Nell never could get anything straight. She's always had it in for me."

Fred jumped up off the couch, nearly falling forward.

"That's damn well enough, Mabel! Get back over here and sit down. And quit shaking your blasted finger!"

Mabel whipped her head around, eyes reduced to penny-thick slits, and mouth splayed open like fresh roadkill. "Don't you dare talk to me like that, Fred Castle! Keep that up, and your old ticker's going to explode!"

"What? Explode like your mouth? I can't get a word in edgewise with all your damn commotion!"

Ann tapped the side of Sarah's canvas sneaker with her shoe.

Eyes wide, amazed by her father's rare display of gumption, she said in a whisper, "Wow!"

Sarah bobbed her head, silently mouthing her encouragement. "You go, Daddy!"

Fred plopped back down on the couch as if receiving a solid blow to the head. He tried to calm himself by taking long, deep breaths. And after wiping his damp brow across his sleeve, he gazed at Mabel, patting the cushion next to him.

"All right, come sit ... please. Let's start over again. I'd like to speak."

With a vexing sigh steeped in sarcasm, Mabel tossed both hands in the air.

She shook her head, eyes closed.

"Have at it," she said, pushing Sassy from his spot on the far end of the couch and taking a seat, left side childishly pushed against the arm of the sofa.

The three women waited in silence for Fred to speak, each gazing off in a different direction as he rubbed the bridge of his nose, eyes closed.

"Ann Marie, before we brought you home, we were advised of the trouble an adoptive couple at Rhineholdt had had with their two adopted kids ... both kids learned of their adoptions at an early age."

Solemnly, he folded his hands in his lap. "The boy ran away a number of times before he turned eighteen years old ... and the girl ... well, she became pregnant and ran off with a ... low life. And not wanting something similar to happen to you, we decided not to tell you about your background."

Fred glanced at his stone-faced youngest daughter. "The same, of course, Sarah, goes for you. Right or wrong, it's what we did."

Another long silence weighed on the thin, high-country air.

At last, Ann shifted around in her seat and broke the stillness.

"Sarah, I have to ask Mother something that's been bothering me since I was a kid."

"Of course." Sarah squeezed Ann's knee, her eyelids drawn.

Ann wrapped her arms around her middle and leaned forward, legs crossed.

Glaring into Mabel's taut face, she asked, "Why do you like Sarah so much more than me?"

"How can you even ask such a thing? I've never liked Sarah more than you. I love both my children the same. You know that," she said, her tart expression saying otherwise.

"That's not true, Mother. And it's obvious to more people than Sarah and me."

"What? No!" Mabel scooted to the edge of the cushion, face glowing crimson.

"Yes, I'm afraid it is."

Sarah dipped her head and patted Ann's shoulder.

"I want to know why? What have I ever done to you, Mother?"

"Okay, Ann Marie. You want to know why? Well, here goes: It's Sarah's big personality. It shines!"

The corners of Mabel's mouth turned up slightly, and with a hint of pleasure in her voice, she continued, "I've always liked her personality more than yours. Hers is everything that yours is not!"

Donning a full-fledged smirk, she added, "Then, of course, there's your hunched back!"

Ann stood and faced both her parents while willing her sweating limbs to stop shaking. "Finally. The truth." She turned toward Sarah. "I'm through. I'll be out in the van when you're done."

"One more thing, Ann Marie … and you may want to sit back down for this one," Mabel said, tone harsh.

"What?" Ann stood, feet rooted in the worn carpet.

"Did your dear aunt tell you that we all traipsed off to the adoption agency together because both of us couples wanted to adopt a baby? And that they had first dibs on you?"

She dug even further.

"Did she let you know that when the paperwork came back from the adoption agency, they claimed your uncle was too old to adopt an infant? Did she tell you that's why we ended up with you?"

Ann felt the room reel like a boozy bad dream.

"I've gotta get out of here before I'm sick!"

"Wait, I'm coming with you, Annie," Sarah replied sideways. "But I have one more question for Daddy." She stood up and looked at Fred. "Are we from different biological parents?"

"Yes," he said, slowly nodding his crestfallen head.

Sarah turned to follow Ann. "Okay, let's go."

With sudden urgency, Mabel rose from the couch. "Wait, Sarah, you'll still be coming home for Thanksgiving, won't you?"

"For chrissakes, Mom, let me get through the rest of this day before I answer that question!"

The sisters zigzagged like lightning bolts through the kitchen and into the dining room, plucking their coats off the back of the chair before heading outside into the frigid evening air. When she reached the van, Ann turned toward Sarah, who leaned against the driver's side door.

"Wow, Mother's parting shot kicked my butt ... like I bet she knew it would!" Ann clasped her hand over her mouth and bent over, coughing. "It feels like she punched me in the gut ... I can hardly breathe!"

Sarah sidled up to her, patting her back. "It's okay, slow down."

Ann nodded as the two hooked elbows.

Sounding like a cold diesel motor, she cleared her throat. "Sorry ... I must've swallowed saliva down the wrong pipe."

She tapped her chest and took a deep breath. "Oh, Sarah ... I can't tell you how often I'd wished Uncle Bob and Aunt Nell were my parents. I'd have given anything to live with them when I was a kid. They made me feel wanted ... and accepted."

Sarah pulled out a tissue from her coat pocket and handed it to Ann.

"Thanks." Ann sniffled and wiped both eyes dry.

After a few moments of soul-searching silence, Sarah spoke up.

"Annie, I don't want you to think I'm abandoning ship, but I'm gonna have to take time out from Mom and Daddy. How much time? I don't know."

She dug the toe of her sneaker into the loose gravel. "I have to sort this all out. You understand, don't you?"

Ann exhaled, watching her warm breath explode into billowy clouds of white vapor. She replied through drawn lips, "I don't blame you, Sarah. I'd probably do the same if it weren't for Katie and feeling the need to make amends with them before the holidays, especially Dad."

Chewing on her upper lip, she continued, "I have to confess, though, I feel like a cornered rat."

More weighted silence ensued before Sarah gave her sister's hand a tight squeeze.

"I'm still not convinced they told us the truth, Annie."

She rubbed her forehead.

"For all we know, they could've withheld our adoptions from us because, sadly, they felt inadequate that we weren't biologically theirs. Mom, especially. Heaven forbid the world might see her in that light!"

With a shrug, she added, "Maybe it all hinged on the idea of the American dream—prosperous couples with their two children and the white picket fence. Who knows?"

She pulled Ann into an embrace.

"Annie, please don't blame me for Mom's insane comments about our personalities. That's the crazy fool in her talking."

"Yep, it is." Ann tugged on Sarah's arm. "Come on. Let's get out of here before we either put that woman out of her misery or we freeze to death!"

Chapter Eighteen

August 1994 – August 1995

With a forceful sigh that sent Bernie and Gus scattering, Ann turned off the kitchen light and retreated to the living room sofa, a diet soda and a can of Pringles in hand—her first solid food since a piece of buttered toast early that morning.

Ann had already divvied up the casseroles, vegetable trays, and desserts—food given to her family by townspeople offering their condolences—between the kitchen refrigerator and the chest freezer in the garage.

Tomorrow, she'd shuttle several days' worth of diabetic-appropriate meals to her mother and possibly break out her personal stash of thank you notes, realizing Mabel refused to pick up a pen and write congenialities, heartfelt or not.

"My, what a long day!" She placed the soda and chips on the coffee table. Kicking off her sheepskin slippers, she curled up against the arm of the couch, bathing in the precious silence until a burst of loud snores trumpeted down the stairs.

A tender smile brightened Ann's face. "Poor Tim."

Ann knew dealing with her father's death had taken a toll on him, too.

"As usual, boys, he needs to be at the store before dawn," she said to the dogs, who'd started begging. Ann took a fleeting glance at the empty stairway, a landslide of gratitude hitting her head-on.

Thanks, Tim, for helping me get through these last few difficult days. And thank you, Katie and Sarah, for staying with Mother again tonight ... I guarantee you're collecting a bucket-load of good karma right now.

Ann wiped a lone tear from her cheek with her sleeve.

I still can't wrap myself around the fact that Dad's gone ... the melanoma spread so fast. She tried to rub away the giant goose-bumps prickling up on both forearms.

I'm thankful we made our peace.

Gus let out a plaintive whimper, reminding Ann of pending business, while Bernie sat on his haunches, leaning his head against her leg.

"Okay, you two yahoos, it's one chip each and off to bed."

Ann stood up, popped the plastic lid off the can, and shook the first two chips free from the tall stack. She tossed both treats simultaneously, marveling at how Gus practically inhaled his mid-air, whereas Bernie gave his nothing more than a cursory sniff as it touched the ground.

"A minute ago, Bernie Boy, you were begging for one. You and your brother are as different these days as Sarah and me. Kinda like … hmm … Cheetos and charcoal." She picked up Bernie's chip and handed it off to his brother. "Come on, fellas, time for bed." She led the way to the laundry room.

Back on the couch, Ann stuffed chips into her mouth, two and three at a time, as thoughts of today's memorial service drifted through her mind.

What an honor for you, Dad, that the sanctuary was packed full. That says a lot. And it was great that a few of my cousins were there ... Sarah and I hadn't seen them since we lived on the Aurora farm.

Maybe I'll try to keep in touch, Christmas cards, at least, like you used to do.

They say it's never too late to start ... whoever 'they' are.
She took a hurried swig of soda. "Oww, that hurts! Damn brain freeze!" She grabbed her head and waited for the skull-splitting pain to pass.

"Ugh!"

Eyes half-mast, she pressed her torso into the back of the couch and rubbed her temples. "Man, what a wimp!" A half-hearted chuckle rapped lightly on her eardrums.

Dad was so stoic, and here I am whimpering over a stupid brain freeze.

Minutes passed before she caught herself staring sideways at the blank TV screen, a loud, deep yawn nearly swallowing her face.

Fighting sleep, she plucked a framed photo of Sarah, Katie, and herself posing as Charlie's Angels—faces somber, weapons drawn—from the coffee table and traced her sister's profile with her finger.

Oh, Sarah, I know this whole adoption mess pushed you away from Dad these past few years. I only hope you don't allow yourself to get bogged down in guilt.

You darn well know you weren't merely Mother's favorite.

You were his favorite, too. I was jealous that you two had so much in common ... classic cars, good Scotch, lively discussions of current events—

The only thing Dad and I talked about was Katie. But I have a bigger fish to fry, and her name happens to be Mabel ... the barracuda! You're lucky that you get to take off for home tomorrow.

Ann put the photo back and lay down, draping the soft chenille throw over her frame. Then, as if someone had snipped the stiff ribbon from a bouquet of funeral mums, the tension dropped from her body.

Sleep happened in an instant.

■ ■ ■

Despite the best of care, winter's long, sharp claws had kept Mabel pinned to the bed for months on end, first at the hospital in Silvermile and later at her home with Larita Moretti, the compassionate, free-spirited caregiver Ann and Sarah had readily hired in January. Yet in due course, with the gradual rebirth of spring, Mabel's *one-two-three* punch had returned with a vengeance, bringing with it increasing bouts of confusion, anger, and paranoia.

With Mabel, nothing would be easy.

Propped up by a plethora of pillows, her days chiefly consisted of time spent on the family room couch nearest the picture window with the view of the meadow and a cedar-shingled birdfeeder mounted to a post in the foreground.

However, even though tethered to an oxygen tank, when a spurt of spunkiness lit a fire under her feet, she took hold of her walker, steering it along her usual carpeted routes.

As Monday morning broke gracefully across the meadow, Mabel—eyes adhered to the window—spotted a doe with her twin fawns standing alongside the creek bank.

As tickled as a toddler, she whooped and hollered.

Hurriedly, she attempted to slide her feet into her slippers and raise herself up off the couch to fetch her camera from across the room.

"Hey there! Hold on, Miss Mabel," Larita said as she trotted into the family room from the kitchen, coffee scoop still in hand. "What's all the commotion?"

"Well, it's a fine time for you to show up! Help me up off this couch! I wanna get my camera so I can take a picture of the babies!"

"What babies?" Larita asked, bracing the front of the walker with her hips and gently taking hold of Mabel's upper arms so as not to pinch her onion-thin skin.

Mabel's demeanor softened.

"Why the fawns in the meadow, of course. Here, trade places with me so you can see out the window ... the cute little pistols." Larita leaned across the sofa.

"Well, I'll be. There they are with their momma." She straightened herself and followed Mabel over to the desk. "We'll have to name the doe Mabel and the babies Annie and Sarah. How about it?"

"No way! My two darlings want to lock me up and throw away the key! Some night, they're gonna sneak in here and try to take me hostage ... but I'll fool 'em by calling the sheriff on 'em. I even wrote the number down next to the phone."

Biting her lower lip to keep from laughing, Larita brushed a stray wisp of thinning white hair from Mabel's forehead. "Nobody's going to take you away from your house, Miss Mabel." She pointed to Sassy, sprawled out across the foot of Mabel's makeshift bed, indifferent to the hubbub, unlike Rufus.

"Who'd take care of the cats?" Larita continued. "They count on us both being here."

Mabel dipped her head in agreement and motioned toward the meadow, a devilish grin on her lips. "Go outside and get a picture of the twins, would you ... please?"

"Of course, but let's get you back to the sofa first."

Mabel's temper flared up like a wildfire. "I can still move around just fine! Don't you dare take *that* away from me, too! If it's not one thing, it's another. That damn Ann Marie even pocketed my car keys."

She shook her finger in the air like a whirlybird. "But you wait, I'm gonna find out where she hid 'em and go for a nice long drive. I'll be a regular Barney Oldfield."

"Hey, I have a much better idea; how about I take you for a drive up to Loop Lake this afternoon?" Larita waited for an answer as she watched Mabel maneuver her way back toward the window.

"I've been in Clifton for nearly five months and still haven't seen the lake's shores. It's time, I'd say. Yes?"

Shrugging, Mabel answered, "Yeah, I suppose that'd be all right."

"Okay, first, I'm going outside to get that prize-winning picture. I'll be back in a second." Larita removed the lens cap from the camera and set it on the coffee table. "You can hold on to your walker and watch me out the window if you'd like."

No sooner had Larita stepped outside than Mabel put the walker into four-wheel drive and tottered back across the living room to the bathroom, locking the door behind her. "I'm gonna take my shower today by myself come hell or high water!"

Struggling to catch her breath, she wiped a bead of perspiration from her top lip with the back of her wrist.

"Whew!"

With one hand on the walker, she slid her elastic-waist pants down, watching them fall into a rumpled heap on the black-and-white linoleum.

Still struggling to catch her breath, Mabel turned to sit down on the toilet seat and missed, tumbling to the floor. "Help me!"

"All right, I got some great shots," Larita said as she rounded the corner into the family room. She glanced at the empty sofa before dashing to the bathroom door, banging hard. "Mabel, are you in the bathroom? Mabel?"

A faint cry for help carried through the old-fashioned keyhole, but the knob refused to budge. Thinking quickly, Larita ran into Mabel's bedroom and removed a hairpin from the top of the dresser, jimmying the lock open on her second attempt. After a quick assessment, Larita knew Mabel had injured her left hip. She raced to the kitchen phone and dialed 911.

■ ■ ■

As promised by the animated weatherman with the Southern accent on KUSA-TV's early morning newscast, a cellophane-clear afternoon had materialized, the temperature a pleasant seventy-four degrees. Larita loaded the last of her belongings into the deep pouches of the studded leather saddlebag attached to the back of her Harley.

"Well, Annie, I better head out if I'm going to miss Denver's hellish rush-hour traffic," she said, adjusting her black leather chaps. "I'll keep an eye on the time and send good thoughts your way at two o'clock." She shook her head. "I hope you understand that I don't do funerals. Never have and never will."

Ann nodded. She grabbed Larita's hands, giving them a firm squeeze. "Thanks, my friend, for everything. You've been such a bright spot in our lives ... Tim's, Katie's, Sarah's, mine, and, of course, Mother's."

She chuckled. "I swear your halo grew bigger and brighter with each passing month you spent with her. You truly have the patience and wisdom of a saint. As corny as that may sound."

Larita pulled her long jet-black mane into a ponytail and laughed. "Well, she was an ornery old mule and as spunky as Sassy on a catnip high ... definitely a handful!"

"Yeah, the first time she'd have thrown her walker at me, I wouldn't have thought twice about giving her the need for another hip replacement." Ann's silliness brought forth a hint of a smile. "Seriously, though, I'm amazed at how fast she went downhill after her hip surgery. Seems lots of old folks' bodies don't bounce back after being cut into—the beginning of the end."

"And now marks a new beginning for you, Miss Annie!" Larita wrapped an arm around Ann's shoulder and gave her a gentle shake. "Which reminds me of a saying in the book of cowboy quips your mom kept by the downstairs toilet. It read, 'Don't squat with your spurs on!' Remember that book?"

A look of confusion washed over Ann's face. "No, sorry. I don't follow at all."

"Well, if one prods a bit, that saying is pretty good advice."

Larita placed her hand on Ann's shoulder. "Don't let the pain of the past keep poking you in the butt, Annie. Remember that the past makes a splendid teacher. Claim this lesson, learn from it, and proceed one hundred percent into the present. There's always good to be gleaned when you're willing to dig for it."

She stepped back, removed her helmet from the handlebar, and placed it on her head, adjusting the chinstrap.

From her back pocket, she produced her black leather gloves, slipping them on.

"Come here, you," said Larita, motioning Ann over and planting a kiss on her cheek.

"At the least, I'll be back every so often for a Gus-and-Bernie-fix," she added, swinging her right leg over the seat. "You can't get rid of me that easily!"

Fighting back tears, Ann waved.

Larita revved the engine and shot past Mabel's wobbly metal gate.

Same goes for me, my friend.

You've made such a big impression on me in such a short time.

You're Uncle Bob incarnate, that's for sure.

It's not going to be the same around here without you ... or ... Mother, for that matter.

She turned around and looked toward the house, half expecting to see Mabel's dour face at the kitchen window.

I wish things would've been different between you and me, Mother, but it wasn't part of the 'game plan' ... there was no ... 'team victory' to be had.

A smile as wide as the creek below slid across Ann's face.

Hmm, maybe it's true ... maybe I'll have to make 'new moves' ... look at the whole thing differently. Suddenly, she surprised herself with a carefree, breeze-in-your-hair laugh. *Listen to me and my 'game analogy.' No doubt about it; a little of Larita's rubbed off on me!*

Ann looked at her wristwatch and darted toward the truck, arms pumping back and forth. "Oh, no, I gotta get going!"

Hurriedly, she placed her right foot on Bubba's wide running board and pulled herself up by the handhold, careful not to catch her long black skirt in the door.

On the way to the church, Ann made a slight detour, wheeling the truck up to the outdoor mailbox at the brick post office. She picked up the thick business-sized envelope next to her on the seat, closed her eyes, and held it over her heart.

"This is it ... no turning back now."

After taking a deep, calming breath, Ann stretched her torso out the driver's window and shoved the lengthy court application to search for her birth family through the opening. With great excitement, she listened as the envelope bounced off one side and then another with a *thwack, thwack* before landing on the heap.

What's Larita's quirky saying? 'Chances taken; what-ifs shaken'? I know this is the right thing to do. I feel it in my gut. Something good lies ahead. If we're receptive to it, that is.

Right, Larita?

Epilogue

September – October 1998

Ann barely heard the phone ring over the high-pitched whine of the vacuum cleaner.

She tapped the power off with her barefoot and propped the metal wand against the sofa. "I'm coming!" she said, darting across the living room carpet and onto the smooth kitchen tile.

A quick glance at the incoming phone number revealed Aunt Nell's area code.

Oh, thank goodness, I'm glad she came to her senses! I still don't understand why she thought I'd replace her with my birth family once I'd found them.

I love that woman to pieces!

Ann pushed the 'talk' button. "Hi, Aunt Nell! I'm so happy—"

"Hello, dear. I'm afraid this isn't your aunt Nell," said a frail female voice.

"Huh?" Ann took another look at the caller ID.

Oh, yeah, the rest isn't Aunt Nell's phone number.

"You must be Ann Palmer. My name's Becky Kirkpatrick. I'm a friend and neighbor of your aunt's or, more exactly, *was* a friend of your—"

"What? Where's Aunt Nell?" Ann asked, a frown wading up her forehead.

"Ann, I'm afraid I have bad news. Your aunt passed away last

Monday, the fifteenth. She'd reached the point where she'd given up her cancer battle. She'd ... quit treatment ... stopped eating—"
"*Cancer*? What're you talking about? You have to be mistaken." Ann leaned her full weight into the kitchen island. "You've dialed the wrong Ann Palmer; I'm certain. You can't be talking about Nell Meyer."
"Yes, honey. I'm not surprised you didn't know. She told me she'd shared her breast cancer news with only a few people—her hired hand and a few neighbors, me included. Most of her longtime friends had already passed away."
"This can't be real. I ... don't believe it."
Sniffling, Ann wiped away a tear. "When's the funeral? I wouldn't miss it for anything."
"Oh, my ... the service was Friday, three days ago. I'm so sorry!"
Ann groaned. "Please ... will you at least tell me why no one notified me before now?"
In little more than a whisper, Becky replied, "Unfortunately, no one knew she even had a niece until this morning when I found your contact information tucked inside her family Bible."
"She has ... rather *had* ... two nieces. I have a sister, Sarah."
"Goodness' sake, Ann, my condolences to you both."
Becky cleared her throat.
"There's one more thing. Below your contact information, your aunt had written, 'In our hearts, Annie, you were *our* daughter.'"
Before Ann realized what she'd done, the call ended.

■ ■ ■

The next few weeks pressed hard upon Ann's shoulders. She considered why Aunt Nell had balked at the thought of her searching for her biological family and concluded that her aunt had lost her once to Mother and Dad and wasn't about to lose her again to total strangers. So between the bittersweet sting of Aunt Nell's death and the agony of waiting to hear that a court-appointed intermediary had begun the search, she found herself, for the first time, robbed of focus.

Katie thrived in her big-city job in Seattle and called less and less, and what with cutbacks at the market, Tim found himself working more.

Too much free time had become her adversary. She'd boxed up the leftover photos months ago, and writing additional family stories no longer interested her.

Lately, Ann found herself fabricating excuses not to attend church, meet with friends, or grab the occasional cup of coffee with Sarah.

So, when she agreed to Larita's request to stop by, she surprised herself.

Up early, Ann straightened the house, took a bag of oatmeal raisin cookies out of the freezer to thaw, and readied the coffee maker.

Then, like the first school bell of the day, Larita arrived on time. Expectations morphed into surprise as she glanced out the front window.

Wow, Larita's driving an SUV, a red one! And she cut her hair!

Ann's face lit up as she opened the door. "Well, I'll be. Look at you!" Wasting no time, she pulled Larita into a fierce hug.

"My, my, it's been way too long, Miss Annie."

Bernie and Gus, their tails moving in double-time, ushered their former walking buddy through the doorway. The two friends sat down next to each other on the sofa, sinking back into the cushions, their knees nearly touching.

"A little birdie told me you might need cheering up."

Ann laughed. "You must mean a *big ostrich*!"

"Well, something like that anyway," Larita replied with a caring smile and a chuckle. "Tim's been worried about you, Annie."

"Ugh, I know. This isn't like me."

Larita gave Ann's shoulder a squeeze. "Sometimes, all we need is a nudge in a different direction."

"And you're about to give me that *nudge*, right?"

■ ■ ■

As Ann studied the local community college's fall catalog, jotting down course titles and numbers, Tim handed her a bulky envelope and the brass letter opener off the desk.

"You might want to take a look at this, Annie; it was sent from the Plummet County Courthouse."

Her hands trembled as she ran the letter opener underneath the top flap. "Please, Tim, would you read it to me?" she asked, handing him the handwritten cover letter.

"Sure."

October 20, 1998

Hello, Ann; my name is Kathy Bellows.

I am your appointed court intermediary.

It is my privilege to tell you that I have already located and spoken to your biological mother. She would like to begin contact with a telephone call.

Before you place a call, however, she wanted you to know

that you were conceived as a result of stranger rape, and even though this was the case, the decision to relinquish you was a difficult one.

Her age—she was forty years old at the time of your conception—and the fact that she was a widowed mother of a teenage daughter were the main reasons for your relinquishment. I also want you to know that she remembered your birthdate and said you have always been in her thoughts.

Tim stopped reading and stooped over to catch the tears sliding down Ann's cheeks. After a long moment, he once again glanced at the paperwork. "The rest is contact information, a medical history form for your birth mother to fill out, etcetera."

"What's her name, Tim?"

Ann held up her palm as if to push him away.

She smirked and shook her head. "Just please don't tell me it's *Mabel*. Promise me?"

With a note of amusement, he replied, "Her name's Esther Jean Wheaton."

Ann slowly bobbed her head, a sense of solace wiping away her melancholy.

"Esther. Now, that's a name I can learn to love."

She removed the paperwork from Tim's grasp and took his hands in hers. "The first time Sarah and I met Larita, she explained that the name Mabel was of English origin and meant *lovable*. We both laughed. Not even close! Not *our* Mabel! But the name Esther … will make for a whole different story."

Author's Biography

The Broken Turtle Blues is Ruth Maxwell's first novel. Her short story entitled "The Broken Buffalo" was published in *Valley Voices: Passages – An Anthology of Central Colorado Writers* in 1999. Both the novel and the short story explore similar subject matter.

Ruth and her husband, along with their tuxedo cat and big-eared Chihuahua, live half the year in Ocean Shores, Washington, and the other half in Yarnell, Arizona.